ROBERT'S WING

A fictional reflection of the grit of Americans as
personified by Rhode Island's youth in the Civil Air
Patrol of World War II.

By

THOMAS BRANDY

ISBN: 978-1946195197
Library of Congress Control Number: 2017958944

21 20 19 18 17   5 4 3 2 1

Cover Design by John V. Hagen

Interior design by Fuzionprint.com

ROBERT'S WING

ACKNOWLEDGMENTS

As Young Can Be

When I was as young as young can be
To wear patches
On my knee
I often took pleasure
In following a friend
Who I believed
Was the living end.
He was my general, my star, my preacher.
Without a doubt, my very best teacher.
Yes, to me, he was the very best
Though to him, I was but just a pest.
Still, in all the world there is no other
Who can ever replace
My older Brother

Thomas Brandy

Thomas Brandy

In addition to the continual support, enthusiasm, and interest provided by my brother, Dr. William T. Brandy, I consider it important to mention the assistance I received from the following individuals:

- John V. Hagen, M.S. for his art direction and assistance.

- Robert Dingmann, SYSCM(SS) U.S.N., Retired, for his technical assistance regarding submarines

- Harriet Hodgson, author, for her sincere advice and assistance regarding the format and style of this work and publishing resource options.

- My son, Kyle Brandy, and neighbor, Mariana Suarez for their shared computer knowledge and support.

- Randy Brock, Chief Meteorologist at KTTC TV in Rochester, Minnesota, for his weather history advice.

- The entire reference staff at the Rochester Public Library, for their tireless interest and research assistance.

- My six patient readers for their honest, constructive criticism.

Thank you, one and all!
Thomas Brandy

AUTHOR'S NOTE

"HOPE" The Rhode Island State Flag Motto

To be from Rhode Island is an honor and a privilege. It is a state that not only is a microcosm of our nation but a fiercely independent model for the world. From its beginning, it has been a proud gathering of people from many nationalities and religions seeking freedom. Whether of English, Scot, Irish, Polish, Dutch, French, Portuguese, Italian, African, Asian or Mideastern heritage, it has guided the spirit of our nation's founding fathers to freely act, speak, and worship as they wished. It is what prompted 68 of its citizens to take eight longboats and attack and burn the grounded customs schooner, HMS Gaspee, in the act of war against Britain on June 9th, 1772, a full four years before the rest of the colonies rebelled.

This unique mixture of beliefs packed into the confines of such a tiny state has often fostered keen, spirited rivalries and fierce competition among its diverse groups. While this competition contributed much to the economy and industrial development of the colonies and states, it often surfaced in the form of social snobbery, youthful gangs, town and city rivalries and fierce sports competitions.

Despite the negatives, it is this very same spirit of competition, appreciation, and tolerance of differences that have always been celebrated in Rhode Island and served as America's crucible and role model. It is also what has let it recognize that, despite its fierce independence, Rhode Island is a model for forgetting differences and uniting when threatened by a greater foe.

While Robert's Wing may not have ever existed, its chapters reflect actual incidents and are true to the aforementioned Rhode Island Yankee spirit. Regardless of age, it is what unites all whose ways of life are threatened by a fanatical enemy, whether from outside or within. It is in the very moral fiber of Rhode Islanders, and indeed all Americans, to roll up his or her sleeves and work together for a common purpose.

Robert's Wing is intended to capture this spirit and reflect what is good about our way of life through the lives of the Aero Gang and the very real 65 Civil Air Patrol Volunteers of World War II who gave their lives to stop a silent, freedom robbing invasion. It is in this spirit that this story is dedicated to the People of the Providence Plantations, who continue to lead by example.

MORNING LIGHT

As he climbed to his practice altitude, Robert enjoyed the early morning contrasting light and darkness of the sky as his plane's Pratt and Whitney Wasp Junior engine rhythmically beat flame out of each of its nine cylinders. The buzzing sound of the engine's exhaust was quickly muffled by the wind as it slipped through the wings, wire and open cockpit of his WACO-F biplane, which he had dubbed the Wasp. Robert was always exhilarated by the sights and sounds of his early dawn practice flights over the Atlantic coast of New England. But it was more than the flying. It was really an opportunity to evaluate life and its issues. No matter what the problem or trial he faced, things never seemed to be insurmountable when viewed at 5,000 feet. Indeed, he always seemed to return to earth's daily routine with an improved perspective. Though he never would admit it, he seemed to glean more out of his morning flights than he did from the family's required weekly Sunday church services.

Weather permitting; flying had become a daily, early morning, four seasons, ritual since before he first soloed on December 10, 1939, his 16th birthday. Now, a year later, he was about to turn 17, graduate from high school and decide what he wanted to do with his life. He knew it would include flying but to what extent he wasn't sure. There was a war on the horizon, and he wondered if that would involve him. Part of him hoped it would, but he also wanted to secure his seaplane rating so he could do charter work into Canada and the Alaskan territory.

He pondered these ideas as he put the Wasp through his practice chandelles and lazy eights and other aerobatic maneuvers. Though he had not yet been taught aerial combat, he especially enjoyed the crisp mornings like today with the blue ceiling striped with distant stratus clouds and a closer dotting of cumulous clouds which he attacked from different altitudes. He and the plane seemed to become one, and he just couldn't get enough of this feeling when he flew inverted or felt the centrifugal forces pulling on his harness. He would get giddy and laugh to himself that he guessed he was deeply in love with flying. There was just no other way to explain it!

Love was another topic he occasionally pondered. Was there someone special out there for him to meet? He regretted that he was too shy to get to know anyone from his school life, but he knew he had special feelings for a neighbor of his, even though she was seven years his senior.

A job or college was another decision facing him. How was he going to support himself and someone else if he couldn't find something? He would never be rich flying and pumping gas, and mechanical work at the airport really didn't interest him even though it gave him more opportunities to fly.

He may not have found immediate answers to his concerns, but with each day of flying, he seemed to build confidence that he knew who he was even if he was not certain of where he was going. As he returned the Wasp back to the Rhode Island Coast and lined up for final approach for runway 27 at the Dartmouth field, his head seemed clearer as he mulled the world's current events and conflicts.

Like everyone in his family, he considered himself a self-taught student of history and current events. He knew about Germany's rapid rebuilding of its military following World War I and now its fascist regime under Adolph Hitler. He also knew about the Japanese invasion of China and was certain that both circumstances had the makings of evolving into a war that America could not avoid. Still pondering these issues as he walked from his plane into the ready room to change into his street clothes, he couldn't shake the relatively recent events that made him even more uncertain about his future.

EARLY SIGNS

Captain Hubert Eisenberger was the assigned Kommandat (captain) of LZ127 (the Graf Zeppelin) for her first test flight on 18 Sept 1928. He had watched her construction and knew everything about her. On her maiden voyage across the Atlantic on 11 Oct  1928, the very formal and methodical, chisel-faced captain who enjoyed dressing in his leather uniform and high boots, proudly nursed the Graf up to her mooring at the U.S. Naval Base in Lakehurst, New Jersey. It had been a tough first trip due to high winds that tore fabric off a portion of the tail, but his valiant crew, including his own son, patched her up enroute and completed repairs in Lakehurst.

He continued to stay with the Graf on her Northern Trans-Atlantic flights from Germany to the U.S.A. that occurred on a fairly routine monthly basis (weather permitting) between 1928 through 1931 when she was assigned to a scientific polar exploration flight from July 24 to the 31st. The purpose of this polar flight was to provide scientists and military representatives from Sweden, Germany, Soviet Union, and the United States a platform for meteorological measuring, imaging, and notation of magnetic field change. The mission, however, took on a special meaning for it included the Graf's installation of the latest, German designed, Ashenbrenner Nine Lens Panorama Camera that allowed geo-photographic recording cameras to capture large areas and provide close estimates of depth and altitude of water and landmass.

As the expedition proceeded, Len Ellington of the National Geographic Society noted the precision of the instrumentation, and a U.S. Coast Guardsman was heard to state that he wished that his country had such instrumentation to efficiently discern the shore depths for safe navigation purposes. The lack of a reply, coupled with a rather sinister smile by the photographer, left little doubt that this photo equipment would be just for German use.

It is not known if there was removal of the photographic recording cameras from the Graf and, indeed, if they still may have been present two years later when the Graf flew from Brazil to Miami, Akron, and Chicago to make an appearance at the Century of Progress World's Fair in Chicago. Perhaps she photographed many areas of America as she passed overhead. Following the World's Fair outing, she was assigned to ferry between Germany and Brazil for the next five years. Her North American duties were replaced in 1936 by the newly launched LZ 129 (Hindenburg), which was larger and had better range and speed for the northern route. If the Graf's duties were absorbed by the Hindenburg, and Captain Eisenberger and many of his Graf crew was now with the Hindenburg, perhaps the Hindenburg also had the Graf's panoramic cameras as well. Indeed, her very routes and special assignments put her in an excellent position to document significant landmarks and the depths of our shoreline for possible future infiltration and invasion planning.

Perhaps the best example of this was the famous 10 and ½ hour Millionaires Flight of 9 October 1936 which transported 72 wealthy and influential people on a Fall Foliage Tour along the coast of New Jersey, New York, Connecticut, Rhode Island and Massachusetts and back; an excellent opportunity to photograph the shoreline.

At that time, the Hindenburg sported the new Nazi Swastika on her tail fin, and Europe was sitting on its hands watching Hitler rearm the Rhineland and develop armaments for the expansion of his Third Reich. Having photo equipment on the Hindenburg could have been just a small part of Hitler's insidious plan to take over the world. Her fiery crash of 6 May1937 destroyed evidence of any photo equipment on board. Still, one tends to wonder how U boat captains came by such accurate charts, maps, and pictures of our shorelines as they prepared to hide and then join their wolf packs for their devastating attacks on North Atlantic shipping and espionage assignments in what historians now refer to as The Battle for the Atlantic.

From the time of the Hindenburg crash to the start of the war, Hitler's chief man for the Luftwaffe was General Hermann Goring. He favored the idea of blitzkrieg/lightning warfare and quickly abandoned the Zeppelins which scared Britain so much in World War I. In fact, he seemed to talk down many of the old weapons of the first war including submarines and definitely had Hitler's support in the development of new super aircraft and rockets for launching shockingly devastating attacks that allowed for the slower, more conventional, forces to enter and occupy Germany's enemies. Indeed, when Admiral Donitz requested 300 of his newly designed U-boats, he was forced to accept only 30 initially and modify his strategy of isolating enemy nations by sinking all shipping trying to supply Germany's enemies. Instead, he continually displayed his intelligence and skill by constantly modifying his plans and keeping the allies off balance. Still, it bothered him that Goering had Hitler's ear, and the Third Reich seemed to be ignoring and belittling his ideas, forcing him to make do with fewer men, material, and U Boats. U-87 was one of those few.

U 87

Aside from the Nazi flag she flew when surfaced, this sail tower crew emblem was U87's only other identifying symbol

As he sat in his quarter's desk studying his secret charts and maps, Commander Joseph Bruger appeared confident that his new U Boat was ready for service. It was a Type VII B laid down on 18 April 1940 and completed and launched on 20 June 1941. It had since been on a shakedown cruise in the North Atlantic with the 6th U-Boat Flotilla. Bruger was impressed with his war vessel. Her deck gun could reach out with an effective range of 12.350 meters with a velocity of 700 meters per second. When armed with the 13.9 kg armor-piercing shells, it was an effective alternative to wasting torpedoes. Her other deck gun was a Fluggabwehrkanone C/30 version of the 30/37 flack gun for antiaircraft protection.

In addition to her armament, she was equipped with excellent sonar and radio communications. In the event of damage, she had five of the latest in multiple bulkheads, sealing compartments, and ballast pumps to keep her level and surface, if necessary. She had also been fitted with an extensive, complex and experimental schnorchel (snorkel) system, so she could run on diesel as well as electric power while submerged, if necessary.

Even though Admiral Donitz was granted much less than he requested, the German high command had put a priority on supplies for the U boats. Every available space was crammed with good German sausage, hams, steaks, roasts, potatoes, vegetables, beer, wine, and water. With a crew of 49, half of the sleeping quarters were stocked with food, so the crew slept in the other half on a rotational shift basis. U87 was indeed ready for any protracted assignments, and the crew was anxious to leave the 6th Training Flotilla and head out on her own.

With the completion of many successful test dives and constant crew training drills, Bruger felt ready to be called into active patrols. At the end of October 1941, the opportunity arose when he was given a secret assignment to break off from the 6th and probe the New England coastal waters. Bruger had secret orders to search for isolated locations where the U 87 could submerge but still not be far from land, major industry, and shipping lanes. All of Germany knew that it would not be long before the United States would be entering the war against Germany, and it was U87's job to seek out intelligence, drop off spies, lay mines, and be ready to assist the five wolf packs planned for the area as soon as war was declared.

Bruger's detailed maps helped him focus his attention on the waters off the coast of Rhode Island and Massachusetts. He believed that the Bays of Mt. Hope and Narragansett were target rich for future assaults. Newport had a U.S. Naval Base and a Patrol Boat (PT) torpedo training base, a War College, and there was a US Navy Air Base at Quonset. Bristol had Liberty Ship and PT boat building facilities. Fall River had several large factories such as Firestone and Davol Rubber Plants, Pepperell, and Berkshire Fabric Mills. Providence had large shipping facilities and railroads as well as tool and die plants like Brown and Sharp; all very capable of turning out and shipping war materials. In addition, the area had a large variety of rail, shipping, and fuel depots close to the shore. The trick was to get in, drop off agents, forward the information to Berlin, and plan for future sabotage missions. It was an ideal assignment for the cunning Bruger and his crew.

THE CREW OF U87

Bruger was a proud German and a true professional who had studied and served his Homeland's Navy for years. He was even prouder to be a member of the Kreigsmarine. He was not a tall man but muscular and strong enough to step into any crewman who might argue or threaten. His, by the book, methodical demeanor demanded discipline at all times. Additionally, his brown but graying and slightly receding hair served to enhance his uniform and be an asset in commanding respect from his crew.

First Wachoffizer (1WO) Wallie Jung was second in command to Bruger and very confident that he could captain the U boat should Bruger take ill or be killed or wounded. Like Berger, he knew every aspect of U87. Unlike Bruger, he was more of a Nazi than a German. He was taller than Bruger, and his blond, graying hair made him a dashing example of the pure Arian race that was so desired by the Führer. He was jealous of Bruger's command, and they would occasionally argue and disagree with each other on decisions, though never in front of the crew.

Second Wachoffizer (2WO) Georg Kurtzman was responsible for the crew on deck and the deck gun and flak gun they manned when on the surface. His short brown hair and very muscular body accentuated his youth. In spite of this and his lack of combat experience, he knew his weapons and expected perfection from his crew. He was quick to lead by example, and his bright blue eyes seemed to flash with excitement as he practiced with his crew.

Leitender Ingenieur (Leading Engineer) Dieter Wilhelm was the affable crew member who didn't go in for the saluting and proper protocol. In fact, this short, squatty, balding, often an unshaven man was totally involved with U87. He was a skilled machinist and was always looking to make things better for his boat and the men on board. He even had Bruger's confidence and permission to use his free time to test the experimental schnorchel (snorkel) installed on U-87 so as to allow the sub to run submerged on diesel. In spite of his skills, he was a bit of an eccentric and frequently talked to the different parts of the sub as he made his perpetual maintenance rounds. His lack of formality repulsed Wallie Jung, but Captain Bruger respected Wilhelm's knowledge and experience. The other 48 members of the crew often joked about Wilhelm's personification of the sub to his face and behind his back. He seemed to take all the kidding in stride because no one on the sub doubted his decisions about the boat. It was his boat, and everyone knew it.

Oberstevermann (Navigator) Christian Dillerman was in charge of provisions and supplies and prided himself as the one person on the boat that could speak fluent English and, therefore, the one who would go ashore to map out invasion plans and scout for sabotage targets. Aside from that, he appeared to be rather reserved, if not shy. His rather pale, freckle-free complexion stood out due to his short, slender build, bright blond hair, and hazel eyes. Christian was in his early thirties and seemed always calm except when someone like Wilhelm was being teased or taunted. Not many knew that he had a brother, Franz, who was frequently taunted because he was not as smart as other children his age. Everyone on board knew that Christian was trained and very skilled at hand to hand combat. When he spoke, most of the crew listened. Besides, his calm demeanor made him easy to be liked by everyone.

Oberbootsmann Gustaph Schnippet was responsible for crew discipline and accordingly, was not very well liked by most of the crew. He had a mean, vindictive streak and was quick to try to catch crew members doing something wrong. Often he would jump to conclusions and confine crew members to quarters before he knew the whole story.

The crew called him "Spectacles," or, more often, "Specs," because he seemed to have everyone under his eye. His wire-rimmed glasses and thick lenses, accentuated by his sloping forehead and long sandy hair, which he greased and combed straight back, made him look like the bespectacled rat that he was. He, too, was more Nazi than German, and his only ally seemed to be Wachoffizer Wallie Jung, which more than once posed problems for the crew. When on shore leave, Specs frequently started fights with persons of lesser ability. One time he made the mistake of goading Christian one too many times and, to everyone's joy, "Specs" had to painfully recover in his quarters for several days.

The rest of the crew was seldom seen until a port was reached. They stayed at their duty posts and took pride in their responsibilities. Torpedo men, gunners, and machinists all worked on their instructed precision drills held on a daily basis as the U87 silently approached the Rhode Island coast.

RHODE ISLAND WATERS

At 20:00 hours of the evening of 3 Nov 1941, the watch reported that U87 was entering Rhode Island Sound and observing Martha's Vineyard Ferry traffic. Bruger ordered, "20 meters. Maintain heading."

He called his officers to his rather tight captain's wardroom, located next to his quarters, above Torpedo Battery II, and forward of the control room and radio and sound rooms. He opened his order envelope, boldly lettered **Operation Talon,** and informed them of his decision and how it related to his secret orders. He pointed to his maps as he addressed his men.

"Fellow Kreigsmariners, I have decided to enter Rhode Island waters in a very unlikely spot. We will start to enter Mt Hope Bay rather than the much busier Narragansett Bay. We will surface tonight to charge our batteries and submerge again to periscope depth until we are at mid-channel between the towns of Sachuset on the south and Sakonnet on the north.

We will then surface and proceed into the Saconnet River, which has main channel depths of 19.14 meters. Our surface displacement is 9.57 meters, so it is navigable for us on the surface. Although there is a full moon, the weather has been very warm recently, and I suspect the resulting fog will be our friend. Moon tide is higher than the normal high tide, and that will give us another meter or so depth advantage as to our displacement. Our contacts tell us that the Americans have been very efficient in their clean up after their big storm damage of 1938, and most of the heavy debris was pulled out to sea during the storm's tidal wave itself. The river is not considered a major waterway, but it is deep enough for us to navigate on the surface. There are some very large cavern like areas in the Bay and close enough to shore and should accommodate us and still allow Christian to swim to shore, dress into his fishing clothes, and proceed to survey the area. Jung, your crew can now open the crate marked Trawler Lighting. While in the bay and river, we will look like a returning fishing boat at night. Once submerged, we will also be able to use our periscope for surveillance. I expect us to be in the area for two to three weeks before we leave for combat and mine duties. Any questions, ideas, or thoughts?"

Everyone around the maps knew that Wallie Jung would speak, and all eyes went to his red face. Not only was he angry that Bruger had not included him in his mission plans, but he also felt strongly that Bruger was putting U87 at risk and peppered him with questions.

"How will we explain our presence inside the borders of a neutral nation if caught? What assurance do we have as to the accurate depths of the river or the Bay for that matter? How do we know that there are caverns sufficient enough for our length and width? The river is narrow, and we could easily be seen from either shore," Jung screamed.

To this Bruger calmly replied, "I have explained our plans for secrecy with trawler lighting and fog cover. I am also most confident that my research of the charts, maps, and Berlin's intelligence, derived from Zeppelin photography, is extremely accurate. Moreover, I am very confident in my crew's ability to navigate the bay and river and slip into position unobserved. If we are unable to submerge in the river area, we can drop Christian off and find safety in the deeper bay area or Rhode Island Sound. Either way, we will succeed. Are there any other concerns?"

No one said a word. Bruger dismissed everyone but Jung and, as the crew retired to their respective duty assignments, a few could hear the muffled, vocal exchanges between the two men.

A FOG PROTECTED TALON

It was midnight before U87 quietly surfaced. As predicted, there was a rather thick fog which limited their visibility to about a quarter kilometer. A quartet of distant fog horns interrupted the stillness of the night. The moon could be seen trying to come down through the fog, making the immediate area fairly clear. High tide was underway. Three crew members stood at the bow; two with port and starboard sounding ropes and one with radio and signal flags for immediate communication of depths and direction, if needed. In addition to his charts and shore lights for identification, Bruger experimented with his new sonar sounding equipment to check depths with his men on the bow.

On the surface, U87 could only progress at 4 to 8 km/hr. using one of his two BBC CG UB 720/8 electric motors, but Bruger felt confident that it was enough to proceed against the Sakonnet's flow of 1.8 to 7.4 km/hr. Besides, on the surface, one electric motor was quieter, and if all went as planned, it would only take U87 a little over one fog protected hour up the 3.22 km to 1.21km wide river before it settled quietly to the bottom of one of the two suspected 15 to 24 meter deep caverns off Tiverton. Most of the rock outcroppings and sandy shoals were on the south side of the river, so Bruger steered the sub to the right of the channel which consistently registered 10 meters at its shallowest. With a displacement of 9.57 meters, the sub had a draft of only 4.57 meters, making it tight but possible if they did not run into any shoals. He knew from a 1911 U.S. Ocean Coastal Publication the way to navigate the river, and he chose the 1 o'clock (01:00 hours) high tide time. The extra moon high tide depth gave Bruger the margin of safety he needed.

Time seemed to pass slowly for the crew as they passed what they believed to be High Hill Point, Foglant Point, Sapowet Point, and Gould Island. As they proceeded up the Sakonnet, their progress was slowed by a new and unexpected floating pipeline stretching about 200 meters from the deeper channel of the Bay up to the Balboa oil tanks on the shore.

Without hesitating, Bruger ordered one of his crewmen over the side with an underwater light to see if there was a service channel to the bay so the sub could steer around the pipeline and either continue on into the bay or proceed up the Sakonnet. After about 15 minutes, the swimming sailor returned with a favorable progress report. There was indeed a dredged service channel for the pipeline, and because the line was a floating platform, it could be pushed either way to easily allow passage around the line to the bay or back up the river. After another 45 minutes, they had, at last, made it the 16.9 kilometers from the lighthouse and were over the first cavern.

Soundings by the sonar and the men confirmed the depth in excess of 50 meters. But the length and width were uncertain. U87 had a height of approximately 9.5 meters, and the depth of the depression still gave her a substantial margin of safety, should a skiff or fishing boat pass overhead. Knowing the spot was long and wide enough was critical, however.

Georg Kurtzman volunteered to go over the side and check to see if there was enough room for the 67.21 meter by 12.6-meter boat to settle into her nest. Bruger agreed, and Kurtzman silently slipped overboard with a snorkel and an underwater light. It took him five dives, but in less than 30 minutes he was back with good news.

"We have well over 20 meters on either side!" Kurtzman exclaimed between gasps for air.

Bruger was impressed with the news and ordered U87 to settle into the very large granite canyon which, as planned, would provide the necessary, temporary, pocket of security. At 0400 hours, a slim radio antenna slipped above the surface of the Sakonnet River and sent a message to be relayed to Berlin.

"Talon Down"

THE AERO GANG

It was Friday, the 7th of November, and a group of young schoolboys was approaching Haskins Avenue in the town of Tiverton, Rhode Island. They were taking their usual shortcut, diagonal path, through a baron, grass field on the south side of the entrance to the avenue. Since the weather continued to be unusually warm, they had decided to skip taking the school bus, tie the arms of their light jackets around their waists, and walk the four miles home from Ft. Barton School.

This was their usual habit on Fridays, regardless of the weather, because their pilot friend, Ernest (Ernie) Gibson, opened his cabinet and furniture repair shop so the Aero Gang could have their weekly, rather secret, flying meetings. Six years earlier, the boys had stumbled onto Ernie quite by accident when he noticed them walking by his shop carrying some flashy kites they had made at school. There was an immediate, mutual attraction between Ernie and the boys but a bit of cautious concern from the parents of the boys who worried about an older man who seemed to want to be with their boys. The parents had a meeting among themselves and with the leadership of William S. Branner, an experienced Boy Scout leader; a plan was devised for a rotating adult den leader concept to help Ernie with the needs of the children whenever they scheduled a meeting. In this way, the parents and adult friends of the boys slowly got to see how well he worked with the boys, and soon they knew and trusted Ernie. Their confidence in his many skills even extended their trust to the point that many actually bought some of Ernie's cabinet work.

Today it was at least 60 degrees out and a fine opportunity to be outside with Ernie to talk airplanes and flying. Ernie's place had been a tavern at one time. It was what the locals called a Quonset hut design, which was built like someone had laid a giant half pipe on the ground. The metal roof arched about 60 feet from one side to the other, and it stretched back at least 100 feet. At each end of the tube was a more conventional wooden wall with doors and windows, and the roof of the tube had several skylights built in on alternating sides every 15 feet or so. At the front entrance, to the left, underneath this tube, was a small, glass-topped business counter and three wooden two-drawer filing cabinets. To the right, there was a large pot-bellied coal stove which pretty well heated the entire area when the weather called for it. Most of the time, though, Ernie liked to leave the building doors and windows open to catch the land and sea breezes, which helped dispel the sawdust while allowing a variety of curious birds to fly in and out. Ernie always seemed to enjoy the flying abilities of all birds of flight.

Further back, Ernie had a large number of woodworking tools including two lathes, a large mill saw, two joiner planes, a bench sander, and a couple of drill presses. On the walls, he hung an assembly of wood clamps, glue, and hand tools used in his craft. To the left, half way toward the back of the building, he had a neatly piled assortment of different types of woods used to make his cabinets and furniture. To the right of that hung a large 30' by 30' by 15' canvas curtain which hid his special love, an amphibious 1934 Gruman JF Duck float plane that he had found for a good price and was resurrecting after being damaged in a crash.

Scattered around the plane were tables and about a dozen chairs for the boys to use for their meetings. At the back end of the building, was a large garage door which Ernie used for shipping and receiving as well as a hanger entrance for his plane. To the right of the door, was another 30 x 30 ft space where Ernie had cut an old tavern bar in half and positioned each half about 20 feet apart. He used the resulting two surfaces as a workbench platform to re-fabric wings, tails, and fuselages of the planes and occasional boats that he repaired.

Although not a member of the Aero Gang, Ernie definitely was its leader. He had been a pilot in the Great War and was wounded;

taking shrapnel in the legs and losing an eye that was replaced with a matching glass eye highlighted by a rather noticeable scar from his eye to just behind his left ear. Now, at forty-four, he was trying to make a living, yet still stay connected to his love of flying. He and the boys had been doing their ground school for several years, and he had graduated Robert Branner, Tommy's and William's 17-year-old brother, to actual flying lessons with him. It was just what Ernie needed to feel whole again. At first, he was willing to interrupt his work schedule to help a youngster fashion a kite, glider, or model plane. Then, in the two years it took for the boys to learn flying fundamentals and get to know him, it only seemed natural to say yes to the Aero Gang when they asked if they could meet at his shop every Friday after school. Friday afternoons were good for Ernie as that was usually a time when his orders were filled, and work slowed. For the boys, Ernie's shop was not far from the one-story red brick and grey slate roof blob of a prison-like building, commonly called Ft. Barton School, and a nice way to break up the four-mile walk home.

Despite his glass eye, deep facial scar, and slight limp, Ernie was a rugged, handsome man. He had high cheekbones, and his sandy blond hair was starting to look frosty in places, but this seemed to enhance his rugged appearance. His willingness to laugh at things, especially his own mistakes, made him more endearing to the boys. One only had to meet him once, and he remembered one's name and offered instant friendship to all.

Although the gang really didn't mind that Ernie did not seem to have a family, they all noticed that all their mothers talked about him and wondered why such a handsome man had not met someone. Widow Tarbert seemed to be the most interested, and the boys thought that Ernie might be as well. Mrs. Tarbert's son, Harold, was a member of the gang, and he and Ernie seemed to be close.

HAROLD

Actually, Harold was one of the smartest students Ernie had ever known. Early in his training, he quickly absorbed such flying concepts as the angle of attack, stalls, navigating by section lines, pattern altitudes, and how to set an altimeter. When the boys flew kites and models, Harold was always the first to get aloft. He also took pride in his fitness and could outrun and do more pushups and chin-ups than anyone. He seemed to be a natural at flying and was anxious for more training. Though he always was careful and feared mistakes, he was anxious to start and talked about going to Canada to enlist in their Air Corps, once he had his wings. He, in fact, was so intense that if he couldn't talk flying, he would withdraw from conversations with people, especially girls. A bit of a silent rebel, his favorite color was black, and he usually painted his models and kites black. He liked black shirts and turtlenecks and black pants and shoes. In the winter, he would don a black leather jacket and black stocking cap. This fact, together with his shiny black hair and steel blue eyes, seemed to accentuate his milky white baby face complexion, which only reddened when someone like his classmate, Anna Halloway, would try to talk to him.

DAN

Another gang member who liked talking about airplanes and flying was Danny Lopez. That is except when food was mentioned! Food was always foremost in the mind of the 16-year-old, and his short, pudgy legs always stepped double time to the rest of the gang's and faster still when there was food at the destination! Danny's nick-name was TC because he was a little on the plump side and had two chins. His mom was no longer around, as he lived alone with his dad but had other relatives in the area. No one ever knew his mom, but most suspected that she may have been a Negro because even though he had his dad's features, Danny's skin color was much darker and his long, dark brown hair was heavily greased to minimize its naturally curly tendency. He was the opposite of most of the gang in that he was loud and somewhat of a braggart.

Danny was quick to volunteer before he knew what he was in for and claimed that he knew things when he really didn't. To his credit though, he was not afraid to try things, and the gang knew they could count on him to volunteer—for anything. One time he climbed to the top of a telephone pole to test a signal mirror they had made, only to get stuck near the power lines and drop the mirror in order to climb down. He also tested their homemade parachute by jumping off a 100+ foot cliff above the bay. A gust of wind grabbed his chute and pulled him out over the water. The other boys all laughed for weeks after seeing Danny standing, but stuck fast, in about 3 feet of soft shoreline goo created by the low tide. He was indeed a natural comedian and a good sport that would do almost anything to help the gang and make them laugh. The real chance of his ever completing ground school and dual and solo flight time for a license was rather doubtful. Still, everyone in the gang had a role to play, and Danny's job seemed to focus on getting plane, pilot, and gear ready for flights and possibly becoming a future mechanic.

Today was a special day, as it was Bill Branner's 15th birthday, and the boys, Ernie, and Branner's neighbor, Caty McArdells, had offered a surprise party for him at the Hummingbird Restaurant, where Caty waitressed and cooked. Caty was also one of the neighborhood babysitters, and all the boys loved her, not just for her great cookies and other snacks that she usually carried with her, but for the sincere kindness and caring that seemed to ooze from her always smiling face that was shaded by her graying black hair and highlighted by her wire-rimmed eyeglasses. Not all the boys liked her hug first, talk and eat later demeanor, but they endured because they knew that Caty was Caty and she wouldn't change. If she liked you she would pull you into her bosom and give you a big hug and loudly state, "Ain't he cunning?" She especially liked to serve as a den leader for Ernie's Friday Aero Gang meetings, and even Ernie accepted Cady's hugs, to the laughing delight of the boys.

All the boys were now in good spirits and joking as they left Caty and Ernie at the Hummingbird and walked along the well-worn, diagonal shortcut path toward home. Bill saw his little brother Tommy over at Joe's Fish and Chips stand at the northeast corner of the field, right at the beginning of Haskins where it joined Hwy 138. With TC leading the way, the boys changed their direction and walked over to the shed hoping that Joe would honor Bill's birthday with an offer of a large paper cone overflowing with French fries, or chips as Joe insisted they be called. Danny had been quick to let Joe know about Bill's birthday, and Bill offered a generous sample of Joe's chips to each of his friends. Tommy had been standing by the shed with his friend Toby on their almost daily visit with Joe and any customers that might have a craving for his fair. Today they had met a fisherman named Christian, who had smelled the chips and said that they would go well with the fish he had kept from his day's catch. He was just heading for his boat at the end of Haskins and saying goodbye to Joe and the boys, as the gang approached the shed.

"Never seen him around before. Who was that guy, Tommy?" asked Bill.

Tommy just shrugged, and Joe explained, "He said he was from over by Bristol and has been fishing these waters for a while."

Satisfied with the explanation, Bill opened up his gift again to show Joe, and all the other boys gathered around to have another look.

JOE

The boys didn't really know Joe's last name, but they jokingly thought of him as Joe Enfield because of the James Enfield 003 rifle he had at the ready and in plain sight in the corner of his shed under a red on white banner that said "Our Right to Bear Arms Shall Not Be Infringed". Joe was a veteran of the Great War and had lost the lower portion of his right leg in one of the useless chargers over the trenches that were ordered. He had survived because he had unconsciously continued his charge and, in so doing, packed his bloody stump with good French soil that helped quell the bleeding. The doctors had to cut away more of his leg, but at least he didn't bleed out from his wound. He was given a wooden fitting that allowed him to wear a shoe, but the rather stiff gate that resulted made it difficult for him to get around when he wasn't working. In his shed, though, he took the fitting off and used a crutch which he mastered with great skill and smoothly danced from his fryer to the griddle and back to the counter to serve his customers.

Joe was of Italian heritage and perhaps 5ft 10 inches tall, but the boys were not certain as to his age. They guessed he was in his late forties or early fifties. He usually wore a stern expression on his well-tanned face which glowed under his curly black and silver hair that he generally topped with a dark blue beret. He was a man who had seen tough times but had moved on with a positive outlook. Aside from his love for target practice with his Enfield, his social life seemed to center around the boys. They could tell that he liked them, and they easily returned the favor, especially if they had found or earned some money to buy something. The boys didn't think Joe was married nor had any family, so they would take turns occasionally inviting him to their homes for a meal after work. He usually graciously accepted and because of it was well liked and trusted by the entire neighborhood.

WILLIAM

William Branner was the middle son of the Branner clan and a serious thinker who also enjoyed playing baseball and his accordion. He was the planner for the gang. A rather tall 5' 8" for his now 15 years, Will, or Bill, as his friends called him, was skinny and often sick, with a delicate stomach. He also had asthma so, at times, it was hard for him to keep up with the others in certain activities. Yet, even when he could not be with the Aero Gang at their regular Friday meetings after school, this serious lad, with sunken cheeks, curly brown hair, and deeply set blue eyes, spent most of his free time planning topics for the next meeting. He had an agreement with Ernie to make copies of things the boys needed to become pilots. Such topics as survival, living off the land and water, hunting, fishing and trapping, target practice with air guns, or making survival rafts out of clothing or cushions were usually Bill's ideas. He would find magazine articles and pass them around to his friends to read during the week. Sometimes he'd get his mom to type things on her Royal and ask his dad to run off mimeograph copies at work. Bill would make sure that everyone knew about the topic, announce to Ernie what had been read, and Ernie would guide the discussion and reflect on his flying experiences.

On rainy days, Ernie would pull out 8 or 16 mm films which would deal with the topics that Bill had suggested. The boys liked this because they knew that even when the weather was bad, there would be a meeting, and that meant a possible movie, popcorn, hot chocolate, tea or, better yet, Ovaltine.

TOMMY AND TOBY

Tommy Branner was Bill's younger brother, and although he was not old enough to be a part of the Aero Gang, the toe-headed blonde 5+-year-old pest usually found a way to follow or appear when the boys were in some type of activity. Since their mom and dad both worked at the Firestone plant in Fall River, after school Bill always had to either watch Tommy or let him tag along to the ball field or Bill's friends' houses. During school time, Tommy was either at morning kindergarten or being watched by neighbors, Caty and Bill McArdell or Mrs. Hobarth. No matter who was watching him, he was always game for adventure. He was usually pushing his red Radio Flyer wagon up and down Haskins Avenue almost every day, except real early on Sunday mornings before church when his brother Bill used it to haul his accordion down the street to Anthony Dalessio's house for his weekly accordion lesson.

Tommy's best friend was Toby Glavin. Although he was 12 years old, Toby was not a real member of the Gang either, but, like Tommy, was tolerated by the gang primarily because he was Tommy's friend and Tommy was Bill's brother. Toby was an unusual boy, shorter and slighter in stature than most boys his age. He stood out with his closely cropped, reddish blonde hair, freckle face, and large and slightly buck front teeth. Although he considered himself an outdoorsman and was smart with survival ideas and adventurous, he was a slow learner in the eyes of the school professionals. So, when he did attend school, he was routinely placed a grade or two lower than his peers. He was often teased at school. He did not like being teased and treated like a dummy, so, he frequently was late or truant. Toby also had a slight speech impediment or lisp, and frequently would repeat things

34

that he said. He loved to tell stories that more often were not true, and he would play tricks and joke with people and follow up with an infectious laugh that made others laugh too. He was friendly and pleasant enough but always into things, and adults, as well as his peers, tended to quickly tire of his antics and ignore him. That is, except Tommy. To say that they were friends wasn't strong enough. They were almost brothers and together more often than not—much to the chagrin of both boys' parents. To the Glavins, Tommy was too young and felt concerned with a 5-year-old hanging around with a twelve-year-old. To the Branners, Toby was much too old for Tommy. Perhaps worse, Toby often expressed himself with such off-color vernacular as a moron, idiot, dirty bugger, poopy bagger, and bloody bugger; definitely not good for a 5-year-old to hear.

Still, Toby and Tommy were adventure brothers and, whenever possible, they would slip away from the eyes and ears of their parents to tackle something new and exciting. Each day would start with Toby riding his Rollfast bike to Tommy's and then taking Tommy's Radio Flier to "make the rounds" of the neighborhood. They would usually walk through the Branner's backyard to Zabakie's to look at their homing pigeons and ducks, pheasants, turkeys, and peacocks. There was usually a feather or two to pick up and put in the wagon. Next, they would walk down Hobson Avenue, which paralleled Haskins, and cut through Mr. Hobarth's backyard to talk to him, play with Bubbles, his Boston bulldog, and perhaps be given a peppermint or two while listening to the Red Sox on the radio. Mr. Hobarth usually nursed his Narraganset beer and cheered for the other team as, unlike the rest of the neighborhood, he hated the Red Sox. Mr. Hobarth was retired and aside from listening to baseball and that new upstart kid, Ted Williams, he was skilled at teaching people how to drive cars. For this, he was highly respected, and most everyone in the neighborhood including Mrs. Branner had been taught by this affable, balding gentleman.

Leaving Hobarth's, the two boys crossed the macadam paved Haskins to visit with the Monroe kids. Though they were not interested in the Aero gang, Kendall, Margret, and Jean frequently played with the Branner boys as they grew up together and were still friends. The boys would next go to watch Frank Mortenstein weld or fix something at his little garage shop. Sometimes Toby would accept a blob of molten metal or a discarded part for his collection that he kept in an old tool chest in his bedroom. Then they went next door to Morgan's Dry Cleaners. Mrs. Morgan, who always watched for the boys, had a nice greeting for them and some homemade caramels to die for! Next, they would walk into Corrughdo's Gas Station and Convenience Store at the north side end of Haskins Avenue across from Joe's. Corrughdos usually offered the boys some odd jobs to move boxes or sweep, but that meant a nickel for either a Coke from the machine or a candy bar. They would usually end their rounds at Joe's and offer to help him on the chance that Joe would have some vinegar soaked chips for lunch. Regardless of any award, they always liked talking to Joe, and he seemed to always welcome their visits.

Occasionally, in June and July, the boys would skip immediately going to Joe's and take their wagon across Highway 138 to Pocasset Cemetery, which the boys preferred to call Blueberry Hill. They would spend hours at the many shrubs at the back of the cemetery to fill blueberries in the grocery boxes picked up at Corrughdo's and, though covered with mosquito bites, would return home victorious with enough berries for at least one of Mrs.Branner's neighborhood famous pies.

Following this morning routine, the two boys especially liked to camp and cook at their pretend fort under the secluded umbrella of the tall sumac and wild elderberries, beyond the railroad tracks that bordered the Ford farm, close to the shoreline.

Toby had already taught Tommy how to ride Toby's 20 inch Roll Fast bicycle that had a belt rather than a chain drive. Of course, Tommy's parents felt that he was nowhere near ready to ride a bike, so Toby and Tommy secretly took turns riding the Roll Fast whenever they set out to go somewhere away from 67 Haskins Avenue where the Branners lived.

Secrecy seemed to be the key ingredient for the relationship between the two boys. When Toby wanted Tommy to go swimming at Newport Beach with him, he simply put Tommy in the trunk of his older brother Denny's Ford and kept quiet until they were at the beach. Toby felt that they probably would not have been caught, had it not happened that he and Tommy were spying on two off-duty sailors who were playing kissy face with their girlfriends in the privacy of one of the many grassy sand dunes near the beach. Not wanting to be watched, the sailors chased the boys who ran to Toby's brothers and girlfriend's beach blanket for sanctuary. The sailors explained the situation to Toby's brother, and he and his girlfriend packed up and returned Toby and Tommy back to Haskins Avenue. It was the better part of two weeks before the two got to play together again.

Then there was the time that Toby and Tommy decided to "inspect" the abandoned wells on the Ford farm. Toby had studied the pictures and learned most of the knots in his brother's old Boy Scout manual and, after taking the extra rope from beside the flagpole at Pocasset Cemetery, the two boys took turns lowering each other down the dank, granite-lined shafts below. They even lit rags on sticks and cattail weeds on fire to light the way. The water at the bottom ledge always seemed to be moving, and it tasted better than the tap at home but, after a few similar episodes, Toby got temporarily stuck in one of the shafts. The boys abandoned any further sampling of the water below, and the rope was quietly returned to the cemetery. After that scare, future adventures were limited to the immediate Haskins Avenue neighborhood between Joe's Fish and Chips and the boys' primitive fort under the sumac by the river.

WALTER

Walter Peel was Bill Brenner's best friend. He was a strong, muscular lad who had turned 15 a few months ahead of Bill. They enjoyed playing baseball, swimming and talking about most anything including flying and survival. Under his curly blonde hair and freckled, devilish face, Walter possessed a hazel-eyed intensity in everything he did. Serious and methodical, he would weigh out his options and quickly make mental plans before he would speak or take action on anything. Walter had finished his ground school and was saving his paper route money to log hours flying with Ernie. He was patient though, knowing that he probably wouldn't solo until after he turned 16, and content to bide his time fishing and helping Bill and the younger aero members. As evidence of his love of flying, Walter's garage had several of his ready to fly models hanging from the rafters. Whether it was flying kites or rubber band powered or gas powered model planes, the boys could always count on Walter for assistance. He had a calm way of quietly explaining the principles of flight in a few words, and his curly, blonde head would often be bent over someone else's project before he would tackle his own. His rather shy smile eagerly shared everyone's success and excitement.

D.B.

D.B. was a single, twenty-four year old, attractive brunette neighbor. She usually caught the eye of any male due to her dark eyebrows, sultry, sparkling brown eyes, high cheek-bones, pronounced chin, and, always in fashion, hairdo. With her 5'9" frame, she also had a way of dressing that seemed to accentuate all her female attributes rather nicely. She knew just about all of the Aero Gang because she had been the main babysitter for the neighborhood as she and the boys grew up together. She loved the responsibility of being a den leader and thought of flying as an ultimate goal of her own; saving money for lessons for herself. When she wasn't working, she would stop by the airport in Dartmouth to watch the boys service the aircraft, mow the sod taxi and runways, or fly with Ernie. The boys all had a crush on her and, of course, each one thought she was watching him. The truth is, she had dated Richard Obert, the Branner boys' uncle, but apparently was more interested in some Navy ensign. Still, she liked helping the boys if she could. They had always known her as D.B., or Dee Bee, but were hard pressed if asked what her real name was. She lived in an upstairs apartment at the Burgett's, next to the Branners, so the boys assumed that she was their relative. Still, she was seldom seen with them and would come and go in her burgundy red 1937 Studebaker Dictator coup, which she absolutely loved. It had a hill holder which was a lifesaver when navigating President's Avenue or any of the other imposing steep hills of Fall River. Studebaker was one of the very few standard transmission cars of the day that would not roll back when starting off on a hill. One had to simply put in the clutch and brake at the same time, move the right foot off the brake onto the accelerator, and the car would not roll back and hit the car behind. As soon as the driver would depress the accelerator and bring up the clutch, the car would go forward without rolling back. It was amazing, and D.B. loved to brag about her "Studie," which she called "Baker," to anyone who would listen. She would often be available to take the boys to Ernie's, or the airport. On occasion, she would even offer to let four or five of the gang pile in and go to Bessie's Ice Cream parlor on Highway 138 or, when she went to McQuirs Department Store to shop, so she could show off Baker. Then there were the special times when she would take them to South Park in Fall River to sail their model boats in the knee-deep water of the big, round, cement monument pond. Indeed, D.B. knew how to make any activity fun, and the gang always enjoyed it when she was around. Despite the age difference, they felt she was one of them.

ROBERT

All the gang looked up to Robert Gordon Branner, the older brother of Bill and Tommy. He had recently graduated from Durfee High School in Fall River which was the closest high school to serve Tiverton. Soon afterward, he soloed and earned his wings. Rather than go on to college, he chose to get a job at the airport in Dartmouth, Massachusetts which was about eight miles east of Hwy 138 off of Highland Avenue or about 12 miles from Haskins Ave. He didn't have a car so, on good days, he would either ride Bill's Firestone Pilot bicycle or try to hitch a ride. In bad weather, he would beg rides from anyone in the neighborhood who had a car and the time. More recently, he called D.B. first, since she had a clerical job at Lincoln Park Amusement Center outside of Dartmouth and traveled the route often.

Since Robert was the first Aero Gang member to work his way up the ranks and complete his pilot training, he was highly regarded as a role model and, although he no longer regularly attended the meetings, he would stop in on occasion to encourage the others to stick with it. Robert regularly flew a red, yellow, and black plane that looked like a wasp in flight. He often referred to it as the Wasp. Actually, the 1929 WACO-F biplane was a modified two-seater, so Ernie would recommend a student who deserved a ride along, and Robert would schedule a flight. Of course, Ernie and the gang would make a field trip out of it to watch and learn more. It was also fun for the boys to see which passenger lost his lunch during the flight.

Dashing in his flight suit and jacket, Robert was no doubt the most handsome of the three Branner boys. Even as an infant, he had always had the bright blue eyes and wispy brown hair, not to mention his soft, smooth, ivory white complexion that gave him a reverent almost angelic look that was quick to be admired by everyone and often sunburned in the summer. Now, at 6ft and 170 lbs., this soft-spoken, unassuming young pilot possessed an unconscious demeanor that beckoned others to regard him positively wherever he went. Robert knew that females of all ages were attracted to him, but he never spoke of it and was too shy to even consider capitalizing on it. He liked D.B. and didn't blush and get embarrassed talking to her, but he knew that she was too old for him and, like the rest of the gang, resigned himself to being a close friend. Besides, flying came first, and he could hardly wait until he turned 18 so he could enlist in the Navy or Marine Air Corps and "fly every plane ever made." Until then, he would continue to help the gang and fly when-ever he could.

THE FORT

During the summer of 1941, Toby and Tommy had called it their Fort, but it wasn't much more than a clearing under the shaded umbrella of the sumac trees that hugged the coast just above the seagrass, next to the river, below the Ford farm. Tommy and Toby liked their pretend adventures out on the water in Toby's raft and onshore under the sumac. They were a lot like Tom Sawyer and Huck Finn in that they would go out in the raft, throw a line with a baited hook over the side, and pretend they were out on an ocean far away. They seldom caught any fish except for an occasional Tautog, which was probably the ugliest saltwater catfish ever. Tommy's family wasn't much into fishing, but Toby knew a lot because his family pretty much lived off ocean harvest. He taught Tommy how to dig for littleneck clams by stomping, barefoot, on the shore at low tide and watching the clams squirt through the mud in defense, only to disclose their location for digging.

Walter Peele's Scotch Shepherd, Trixie, enjoyed helping the boys by running to each new squirt and barking, whining, and digging. The clams would then be dug, rinsed off, and put in a sock and kept under water until it was time to take them home. They would then be boiled or steamed and served along with muscles, blue shell crabs, potatoes and sweet corn, when available. Sometimes Tommy's mom would boil potatoes, and along with onions, milk, and butter, make some New England clam chowder with the clams he would bring home.

The depression was still hanging on and any extra food brought home was a plus for any family in the neighborhood. Catches of fish often would be shared by the neighbors be it clams, muscles, cohogs, crabs, striped bass, tuna, or swordfish. Mr. Stephonski (Stephie), Branners' other next-door neighbor, was a very

43

experienced fisherman and frequently contributed most of the latter mentioned catches. Most everyone had a garden for fresh vegetables and any rough fish or remnants after filleting served as fertilizer for the gardens.

Now it was fall, and even though the Gulf Stream always seemed to keep Rhode Island's winters fairly mild and snow never stuck around much longer than three days after a snowfall, this autumn had been exceptionally warm. For Tommy and Toby, it gave them more time to play in their fort. It was 61 degrees on the afternoon of November 10th, and the two boys had already dug out a good size foxhole, but before long they hit the granite rock that was so close to the surface near the ocean. Tommy coaxed Bill, his daytime babysitter from directly across the street, to come and see.

Bill McArdell was Caty's husband and a 60 plus-year-old veteran of WWI who agreed to come down to take a look at what they had accomplished. The boys had heard that Bill had been a victim of gas attack during the war and, aside from occasional walks; he didn't do much but go for drives in his '38 Plymouth and work on his hobby of clock repair. He liked wearing his black, high laced work boots for ankle support and always kept them soft and shiny with frequent doses of bacon grease.

"I am impressed," said the unshaven Bill as he leaned back against the exposed rock ledge and slipped his hands into the pockets of his bib overalls. "But instead of trying to dig down into the rock, why don't you dig a trench further behind the rock so you have solid protection from your "enemy" if they should attack from the water? You might be able to arch around the rock and have another foxhole closer to the shore. If you are really ambitious, you could also run another trench up through the sumac to the Ford farm stone wall. Then you'd be able to avoid detection all the way from Toby's house."

The boys' faces lit up with excitement.

"Great idea! Thanks, Bill!" said Toby.

"You're welcome. But you are going to need some help. That's a lot of digging. I'll check on you from time to time if you want to get started now. Or you could come on up to my place and grab some of my shovels. I'll give you some coffee milk and cookies, so you have some energy to get started."

That was even a better idea, thought Tommy.

Like most of the neighborhood, Bill and Caty McArdell had a neat yard surrounding a white, cape style house with a detached garage. Theirs had dark green shutters and trim, but because they lived on the sunny side of the street, they always seemed to have the curtains closed. Once inside, visitors immediately noticed the ticking sounds coming from Bills clock collection in various parts of the dark interior of the house. A large horsehair couch sat next to Bill's well-worn matching easy chair, both of which filled the living room. The walls were adorned with a Crucifix and pictures of Mother Mary and Pope Pius the 12th. Dividing the living room and the kitchen was a large, upright mahogany piano with a swivel stool which could be turned to the desired height for each musician. Tommy always liked to turn it so he could sit real tall and, even though he knew nothing about music, would offer up a concert of some sort for Caty and Bill, who awarded him with applause and encouraged him to take lessons.

As promised, Mr. McArdell got out the Autocrat coffee syrup and mixed it with the rich milk from the local Bajuma's Dairy quart glass bottle. First, he poured off the thick cream that had risen to the top and used some of the cream for his reheated coffee. He then grabbed the plate of sugar cookies Caty had baked and offered them to the boys with a laugh, saying, "You better help me eat these before they spoil."

As they enjoyed their snack, the boys talked about their fort, and Bill sketched out some plans on a piece of paper for the boys to take with them.

"Tommy, you and Toby can grab some of my shovels from the garage on your way out. Keep them out of the weather and return them clean when you are done. Don't forget to show me what your fort looks like when you're finished."

"You bet, Bill!! Tommy, I'm going to go back and dig some more. You go see if your brother and his friends can help, OK?" Toby ordered.

Bill laughed at their excitement.

"OK!" Tommy answered excitedly as he always liked doing things with his big brother.

Both boys dashed outside to get started; Toby to the back door to get the shovels and Tommy to the front to find his brother. Mr. McArdell continued to chuckle.

Looking both ways before crossing Haskins, Tommy saw his brother turning his Firestone Pilot bike into their driveway.

"HEY BILL!!!" Tommy shouted excitedly.

"What's up?" Bill asked.

"Me and Toby are going to play war games tomorrow, and we need help digging trenches and foxholes."

"In rock?" Bill asked, somewhat amused.

"No, it's soft near our fort."

"Fort?" Bill queried.

"Yea, we've made a fort in the woods, near the river, past the train track."

As they entered their kitchen through the side door, Bill said, "I'm going to have a peanut butter and jelly sandwich. Want one?"

Remembering that he sometimes reacted to peanut butter, Tommy answered,

"Yes, but just jelly for me." While pouring two glasses of milk from their old G.E. refrigerator, Tommy spilled some on the counter but wiped it up with his sleeve before Bill noticed.

Despite his normally serious nature, the war games sounded like fun to Bill. So, after they finished their sandwiches, they left a note for their mom and walked over to Walter Peel's house to tell him about the plan. Walter also liked the idea and grabbed a lunch pail with bread, cheese and peanut butter and jelly in it, placed the pail in Tommy's Radio Flyer, hoisted two shovels over his right shoulder, and the three boys headed down the path to the river where they caught up with Toby.

Toby was sitting deep in the second foxhole he now had dug big enough for himself. He was glistening with sweat on his forehead, and his face was flushed red as he caught his breath. He was happy to see his reinforcements arrive and without much conversation, the boys looked at Mr. McArdell's sketch and started digging the trench system. They dug away at the sandy soil steadily for about two hours, and the end result was two twenty yard by three foot deep trenches to the two fox hole ends with a midway small 8' x 10' fort about 4 foot deep in the sand with a roof of boards covered with scraps of tar paper, rags, cardboard, and newspaper to stop the sand from coming through the cracks in the boards. They had plenty of sand from the trench digging, so most of it was piled on top of the fort roof a good two feet high. They made a door frame and wall paralleling the trench, and Walter nailed up some burlap on the wooden door frame for a door, adding,

"We will need some candles, and I think we can make a small stove so we can use this when winter finally comes."

Tommy had pulled his wagon right into the fort, and Walter pulled out his lunch pail with the bread and a jar of Skippy peanut butter and said, "Let's take a break."

The boys flopped down to make and eat their sandwiches, and Toby passed around a bottle of water he had brought. As they rested, each had a look of satisfaction on their faces. They were obviously too tired to say much.

It was Toby who broke the silence, saying, "When do we fight?"

Walter thought for a moment and said, "The enemy withdrew when they saw our reinforcements and that we were digging in."

That seemed to satisfy everyone, and Bill characteristically added a touch of reality by saying, "Besides, the street lights are coming on, and Tommy and I need to head home. Tomorrow we can bring more supplies, finish our trench path to the stone wall, and start our war games."

Walter added, "Yea, tomorrow is November 11th, Armistice Day! We can fight and remember our soldiers!!" Every one agreed excitedly, and all left for home, except Toby who wanted to sit in his new foxhole for a while. It was not very long before he fell asleep.

Whether it was the cool ocean air, the sand, or a noise, something stirred Toby back to consciousness. He sat up and looked around. It was a new moon and not bright enough to see anything in the dark, foggy night. He did hear a splash and strained to look out past the shore. He thought he saw something in the water and looked again to try to make it out, but nothing came clear through the fog. The tide was coming in, so he quietly slid his raft over the tall shore grass, which was now underwater, and crawled into the raft, grabbing his canoe paddle.

After several minutes paddling the raft into the dense fog, he bumped into something big and metal-- a boat of some sort. "Ohhh, buggers!" he said to himself and quickly back paddled into the fog. Someone was on deck and briefly flashed a light into the foggy darkness, but nothing was seen. Toby noticed that as the man's light hit a part of the boat, there was a scary looking painting of the leg of a bird on the side of the barge or boat. He kept paddling away from the mass of steel as it silently swung around to head down the river.

Toby thought to himself, "Bloody bagger if only I coulda seen what that thing was." He paddled back to the fort, beached his raft, and decided to head for home.

INTO THE TRENCHES

"Can Toby, play?" Tommy asked Mr. Glavin, early the next morning.

"I don't think so," Mr. Glavin answered in a disgusted tone.

"Why?" Tommy asked shyly.

Mr. Glavin appeared to get upset and said, "Because he didn't come home last night until early this morning and is lying to us again about a fort, and a ship, and bird claw legs, and, I don't know what all."

Tommy left all confused and told the other gang members who didn't think anything of it. Toby was just caught telling Toby stories again. So, they simply picked up where they had left off the day before and continued to work on the fort and trenching to the cattle tunnel under the tracks and then up to the wall. Before long, Bill paused to lean on his shovel and said, "It'd be a big help if Toby was here. That kid is a good digger!"

"So, y'all need some hep, eh?" a new voice asked. There stood Swifty, the newest member of the gang. "I had ta track y'all down. I stopped at your house, Bill, and then Walter's and both your moms said you was building a fort down here. Thought I'd stop over to have a look."

"You couldn't have come at a better time. Grab a shovel!" said Walter.

Jefferson Davis Swift, or Swifty as the guys called him, had moved to Tiverton from Texas last year because his Dad had been reassigned to Newport by the Navy. Swifty was a Navy brat who the boys felt was really lucky to have lived in a lot of places. A wiry red-headed, peach fuzzy face kid with an average 5'7" build was soon going to be 16 but was in the same grade as Walter and Bill. He had a thick southern accent when he arrived last year and had

49

since done his utmost to fake a Rhode Island/Yankee accent, but the resulting blend of the two accents was rather comical. Even so, he did not seem to mind all the kidding by the gang that let him be himself. It did not take him long to fit in. He, too, shared the flying bug and had some nice models which he enjoyed showing off and flying with the gang on Fridays. He even got himself into trouble with the Navy when one of his larger models got loose and flew over the neighborhood, trailing smoke and crashing beyond Ford's farm. One startled neighbor lady got a brief glimpse of his plane out of her window and thought it was real. So, she called the authorities to report a downed plane. Before long, a real US Navy Goose buzzed the neighborhood so low the boys could see the pilot's sunglasses, and it scared some of the younger neighbor kids. In spite of a stern lecture from his Dad and a letter from the Navy, Swifty became the neighborhood hero. It was his model that drew in a real Navy aircraft for the boys to see up close and in action! In fact, since he always had his head in a newspaper or flying magazine of some sort, Swifty was the one who seemed to know who had a plane for sale and was forever bugging Ernie and the gang to go to Portsmouth or Dartmouth or even Providence or Boston to look at some available aircraft.

ALONE?

It was getting close to noon and D.B. had walked down to see the boys' fort and, having already talked to each boy's parents, offered to drive them to the Armistice Day Parade in Fall River. They quickly put their shovels away, and each ran home to shower off the sweat and sand. They were long gone when Toby finally arrived at the fort, having, once again, apologized to and been forgiven by his parents for "lying." He was sad that he had missed out on the fun of digging with the gang. He had guessed that they were going to the parade and fireworks, but he didn't really like crowds and chose to check out what the boys had done to finish the trenching and fort rather than try to catch up to them at the parade. He crawled into the fort and sat quietly working on his fishing gear while listening to the sounds of the water, distant shipping bells, and whistles mixed in with the songs of the seagulls and land birds. He looked around feeling as if he was being watched but only saw that it was another nice day, though not as warm. Toby was used to being alone and, like always, started talking to himself.

"I'll bet if I had a telescope or field glasses I coulda saw more yesterday. Maybe if I had a camera, people would believe me." He came out of the fort and went to his second foxhole, checked his raft, and walked back and up the newly dug trench path back toward the Ford farm wall and up to his house. "Oh well, the guys will be back tonight, and we can fight then." Had he looked on the roof of the fort he would have seen the precision made, German, Zeiss field glasses setting there not far from where Christian had been watching him

51

INVASION PLANNING

As he watched Toby slowly heading home, Christian could not help but think of how much he missed his brother, Franz. Toby seemed so lost and alone that the "fisherman" wanted to catch up to him and cheer him up with the field glasses and give him a hug. Still, he thought better of it, left his field glasses, and headed towards the path that took him in the opposite direction, along the tracks, and past the Balboa oil storage tanks. He took mental note of where satchel charges should be placed and moved on toward the highway and to Highland Avenue. He had two days to scout the area before U87 would be surfacing off the town of Saconnet to pick him up. Although near dusk, he thought it best to wait till dark before he headed up Highland Avenue to check out a Forest Ranger Station which was atop the highest point on the peninsula. Instead, he slipped into the cover of some bushes on the grounds of Ft. Barton School. He laughed to himself as he recalled some of the conversations of the boys he had overheard as they worked on their fort. He was surprised to hear some of the stories that sounded vaguely familiar to situations he had experienced in his early schooling. Fort Barton was indeed an imposing building that stood out and looked very much like a fort or place of incarceration. The boys had said that the school was named after a local hero named Colonel Barton who had captured the British General Prescott in the battle for Newport during the American Revolution. They also had talked about the crazy rules enforced by a Principal Dunlevy, who sounded a lot like his Head Pedagogue Schultz. With a laugh, he remembered hearing the HOB (Hands Off Banisters) rule after they were installed. He reflected on how similar children were in both countries but tended to like the more relaxed, fun loving, affect of these American lads compared to the rigid, Nazi youth camp students of his Germany.

Darkness and the ever-present fog soon settled in, and Christian found himself finally climbing the stairs of the forest fire lookout tower. His long hike up the side of Highland Avenue was fairly uneventful, as he only had to slip out of sight into the nearby woods once as a red Studebaker slowly climbed the hill enroute to the nearby town of Dartmouth. Once on top of the tower, he quickly located the above the door hiding spot for the key to the door's padlock, and Christian easily stepped inside. At the center inside of the tower cabin, there was a cluster of a few amenities including a small portable toilet pot with a hinged lid, a water barrel, and a two burner cast iron coal stove that doubled as a small heat source to warm the un-insulated cabin. Next to the stove was a small container of newspaper, kerosene, wooden matches, and a box with a small amount of coal to battle a cold afternoon for someone who would voluntarily man the post during high-risk periods for forest fires. The recent rains and fog put the risk very low, and chances of Christian's presence being detected were minimal. Since it was still in the upper 40's, he decided against lighting the stove. The inside perimeter of the cabin consisted of a continuing series of 24, 2'x4' windows above a two-foot deep wooden countertop about 3 ft high all around. On each side, there were stools and chairs next to the counter and one large telescope which could be moved to different mountings affixed to each side's countertop.

Thinking he would use tomorrow's early morning light to survey and take notes of the surrounding terrain, he decided to use the small cot and blankets. Within minutes he was asleep.

Morning came too quickly, but, after a small snack of the hard bread and canned sardines he had carried with him, he tasted the roof's water from the rain barrel out on the landing. It had a sweet taste of freshness that satisfied. There was still too much fog to use the telescope, so he elected to stay put and wait until the sun was higher in the sky to look around. As he looked down to the base of the tower, he saw a blue 35 Ford pickup truck pulling up to the tower's parking spots with a typical squeaking from its mechanical brakes. An older, stoop-shouldered man with large wire-rimmed glasses topped with a dirty, striped engineers cap and coveralls, got out of the truck, filled a large canvas bucket with coal from a small pile in the back of the truck. He slowly turned, slid the two canvas straps over his shoulders, and started for the stairs. Christian knew what he had to do.

Freddy Zampa was a retired Bowen Oil and Coal delivery man from Fall River. But, even in retirement, he kept busy with some small, but special jobs the company let him do. So every week he would head for Mrs. Almeda's Kindergarten School, Ernie's wood shop, and the reception stove at the airport in Dartmouth. He also checked on the ranger tower for the town of Tiverton.

There were over 200 steps to climb the tower so Christian drew his knife out of its scabbard attached to his shin under his right pant leg and waited till the man was heading up the last series of steps and out of sight to slip over the side and hang onto the girders while the heavily breathing man reached for the "hidden" key, opened the door, filled the coal box, and then sat to rest from the climb. Christian had been able to lock the door and straighten the cot. but then he remembered the sardine can. He knew the smell of the recent meal would give him away. Still breathing heavy from the climb, Freddie sat on a chair resting. He smelled the fish and with a panic look on his face said out loud, "Darn, I should have come here sooner. The volunteers have been here, and they didn't have coal for heat. Good thing it hasn't been real cold though." Christian heard him but kept silently waiting for him to leave even though his arm and leg muscles were starting to shake from the strain of hanging on to the tower structure. At last, he heard the door slam, the key putback and Freddie's slow steps going down. Christian again drew out his knife from the sheath on his lower right leg and quickly climbed back to the landing. He was rubbing his arms with his back to the stairs and looked over to watch Freddie leave. He could not see him until he turned around, and their eyes met. The man's face was reddish blue, and he was holding his chest in pain. "I forgot my bag. Who are you?"

"You don't look too good. What's wrong?" Christian asked instinctively.

"My ticker doesn't like the stairs, I guess," Freddie replied, settling to the floor.

"I'll get you some water." Freddie nodded yes, and Christian bolted to the cistern returning with a full ladle. He knelt down, but the man had breathed his last.

Christian left the man's body where it was and quickly went inside to the telescope and began noting the coordinates of such landmarks as the War College, and Newport Naval Base which appeared to be sitting ducks for either an air assault or an all-out naval barrage from Hitler's superior battleships. He also noted that the beaches at Newport and Horseneck looked like excellent places for an amphibious assault, and the relatively flat terrain around the small airport at Dartmouth would be an adequate spot for advance paratroopers to land. With the Americans having such a weak army and navy, a German Blitzkrieg attack would quickly take over Fall River, Providence, and Boston and allow the Germans to establish a foothold while other units hit the New York and Florida areas. The many, huge, coal-fired electric power plants were not to be destroyed and, though he didn't believe it, the word was that the Third Reich had special plans to eliminate Americans by using them for fuel for those power plants. Christian knew that the final plan was for an eventual pincer movement that would quickly take the east coast and allow Hitler's forces to move inland to the Mississippi in a matter of 3 months.

Christian had personally canvassed most of the areas noted and tried to do preliminary sketches which he intended to elaborate on once back aboard the U87. His day was nearly done, so he double checked the cabin, removing his sardine can, straightening the countertop, cot, and chairs and returning the telescope back to the spot he had found it. He locked the door again and put the key in its common hiding place above the door and turned to look at the coal man's now stiff body. He laid the man's canvas bag next to his body and stepped over him as he started down the stairs. How ironic he would die of natural causes rather than by his hand.

"Too bad. He seemed like a good man," he thought.

Christian slipped down the stairs and into the cover of the protective woods, as quickly as he could while being careful not to move, as a few cars drove up and down the hill. He breathed a sigh of relief once he was again under cover of fog and dusk in the brush and trees behind Ft. Barton School. He rested until it was totally dark again and there was little to no traffic. He then walked to highway 138 and followed it for about three miles, through what the locals called Four Corners until it intersected 114 at the Stone Bridge. He followed 114 for another four, or so, miles to Saconnet and his rendezvous with U87.

He arrived in Saconnet area after midnight and chose to walk along the shoreline, taking mental note as to where he could best enter the water and either row a boat, if he could find one, or swim to the approximate rendezvous coordinates he had agreed to with Commander Bruger. Once he decided on a spot of departure, he walked around the many docks looking for small skiffs he could steal and row to the sub which in the past week, since leaving its sanctuary, had been surveying the Massachusetts and Rhode Island shoreline for future strategic targets.

The water was still warm enough that he could swim in it if he had to, but, he would rather go on board dry for the most part. It was a matter of professional pride, and he knew the crew would respect it. He had accomplished everything he wanted to in the nearly three weeks he had been on land. Now it was the 13th of November, and he only had 20 hours before he would leave. He planned to find a restaurant or tavern that served a good breakfast and then get a room where he could remain unnoticed until it was time to leave. He had been rather successful at stealing money from the homes and businesses he had passed by so he had enough American cash to pay for a good last rest before returning to Germany.

It was only a little blue, and grey 10ft pram with the name Pinky stenciled on the stern, but it was easy to untie and had the oars in it. Once again the fog was on his side, and he slipped away from the dock unnoticed. It was dark and quiet and fairly calm with the distant fog horns periodically overriding the lapping sound of the bay water resisting the rhythmic pace of the oars as Christian propelled his square nosed craft ever further into the darkness. After a half hour of rowing against the incoming tide, he was fairly certain he had reached his correct location which he had triangulated between the harbor spotlights and the distant lighthouse, both of which were faintly visible through the early morning light and fog. He decided to rest for a while, periodically sculling to maintain his position. He pulled out an American Hershey candy bar with almonds that he had purchased at the tavern he had eaten at the night before and enjoyed the rather weak but tasty chocolate refreshment. Right on time, he heard voices due west and began sculling toward the sounds. After about 100 yards he saw 4 or 5 flashlights panning the water, and he soon made out the silhouette of U87. He bid the Pinky a salute as a crew member from the sub used an ax and chopped it to pieces and scattered it to the tide. Within minutes, Christian was in Captain Bruger's cabin for debriefing as the U87 slipped silently beneath the surface and headed home for its beloved Germany.

MILITARY SURVEILLANCE

"Where did you get the field glasses, Toby?" Tommy asked.

"Fort," Toby answered.

"They yours?"

"Nobody else's using 'em."

"Whatcha gonna do wit em?"

"Let's climb your big maple tree in your yard, Tommy, and we can pretend we are looking for the enemy."

Tommy and Toby loved their pretend adventures and started racing across the neighbors' yards to get to the tree. There was a picnic table under the tree and jumping up on that made it easy to get to the first branches and then climb nearly all the way to the top. It was the most fun in the summer when they could hide under cover of the large leaves of the maple, but even with bare branches, the tree was their hideout that served as their plane, ranger tower, crow's nest of a sailing ship, hotel, sniper nest, or place just to sit and look at comic books and chew bubble gum.

Today they were spotters looking for airplanes, and they sat taller than the surrounding houses, creating a great view of the bay, oil tanks, ships, and occasional private, commercial, and navy aircraft. The tree never failed to make it more exciting, as it tended to catch any breeze and sway back and forth. Toby scanned the horizon and made up the name of an enemy B10J heading due west. Tommy pretended to take the report seriously and wrote it down on his pretend paper. Toby then looked out in the bay and reported a pretend barge near their river fort and pretended to call the fort on the "radio" that an invasion force was approaching and that enemy aircraft were in the area. Toby started looking at the surrounding houses for signs of any enemy soldiers in the area when he seemed to stop moving his field glasses.

Tommy noticed that he seemed to be looking toward DB's windows and asked what he was looking at.

"Just looking," he replied. Then he quickly lowered his field glasses with a look of shock on his face, adding, "Oh Oh!"

"Looking at what? What'd ya see?" Tommy asked.

"Nothing," lied Toby, who had just viewed DB toweling dry as she walked down the hallway from her shower to get her bathrobe from her bedroom. Toby thought that she might have caught a glimpse of them in the tree and quickly glanced through his field glasses again only to see that she had discretely slipped from her towel to the bathrobe and had turned, fully covered, and was walking back down the hallway.

"Oh man, I may be in big trouble now!!"

"Let me see!" Tommy demanded.

"No, even if I didn't see anything, I shouldn't have been looking and you really shouldn't! Baggers! I don't think she saw me. OOOOOOh, I hope she didn't see me. I'll never be able to look her in the eye or talk to her ever again!"

"What if she did? She is our friend, isn't she?"

"Yes, but Tommy, we can't admit to anyone that we were looking in DB's window."

"I wasn't." Tommy asserted.

"Neither was I, right?"

"Right," Tommy answered knowing that, if Toby wanted him to keep quiet, it must be important. "We can say we were playing airplane spotter, OK?"

"Yes, but only if we are asked, okay?" Toby stressed.

"Okay. Let's go down to the fort." Tommy suggested.

"Good idea, Tommy." They both scrambled out of the tree as if the branches were on fire.

WAR GAMES

The boys ran all the way to Toby's house to get some bread, peanut butter and jelly, and a quart bottle of milk and Ovalteen mix. Then they were out the door and behind the wall, under the tracks, and into the trench to the burlap door of the fort.

Tommy was the first to notice the stove that Walter had put together. It was from an old Acme four burner cast iron stove with a rusted out bottom. But it had the four good sides, the stove plates, and a door to stoke the fire that worked. Since the bottom rested on the sandy floor, there was no danger of anything catching fire. For a chimney, Walter had fastened together a series of eight paint cans, with both ends removed, up through the roof. The chimney was topped with an old Ford hubcap to keep the rain out. Next to the stove was a small supply of paper and driftwood for burning.

Toby noted, "There's not much wood around here to keep a fire going. We are going to have to always bring some each time we come here. My Dad cuts up old cotton cord tires and burns them in his shop stove. It burns real hot. So, if we see any old tires, we can bring them here and cut them up into small squares for our stove. I'll bring my small hand saw and keep it here so we can cut them for a supply."

"Bet we can find some coal on the train tracks too, Toby," added Tommy

"Good idea Tom. It will be too cold to be here this winter if we don't have stuff to burn."

"Hot Chocolate?" Toby added as he set an old pan out on the stove. Tommy handed Toby the paper and sticks to get the stove started and went out to pick up more wood while Toby lit the fire and poured the milk and chocolate into the pan.

Tommy soon came back with a double armload of wood and noticed the warmth of the stove in their underground room and that Toby was making two peanut butter and jelly sandwiches. Walter had also brought in two old hassocks to sit on at the shortened card table which had broken. Its uneven legs were pressed into the sandy soil to make a fairly level and stable surface.

The two boys sat on the hassocks at the table and enjoyed their first meal in their home away from home. They kept the fire going as, at long last, winter seemed to be creeping in and providing its traditional bone-chilling dampness.

Harold, Walter, Bill, and Swifty had been hunting for small game with their Crossman and Daisy air rifles when they saw the smoke coming from the fort and came to see if everything was okay. They all liked the warmth and how neat the fort felt and joined Tommy and Toby in making some sandwiches.

The four older boys had their BB guns, and Toby had a marble "gun" which was simply a broomstick with a piece of inner tube attached to the tip of the stick. The stick had a loop that could hold a marble or stone and be stretched to let go, launching the respective missiles at a target. Some slingshots the boys had made could be useful for targets at a closer range. Since they were so well armed, the boys decided that today would be a good day to play their war game. Walter also had some firecrackers he had bought for the Armistice Day celebration, so they could pretend that they were grenades and add some realistic sounds to their game. They decided that the next boat passing by would be their signal that they were being attacked and would wait until the enemy would be coming up the beach.

The first to fire would be Toby with his long-range marble gun. He would fire from the central fort area with Walter and Bill manning the left foxhole and Harold and Swifty in the right. Using a slingshot, Tommy would cover the trench to the stone wall so no enemy soldiers could get behind them, should they need to retreat. Walter threw a board out into the water to serve as a target for

Toby and then stuck sticks with newspaper flags attached to represent attacking soldiers on the beach that would be their targets for the BB guns. Then they saw a boat, and Bill gave the command to begin firing, and, as soon a Toby fired his marble gun, Walter set off a package of fire crackers, and the battle was on.

"I'm running low on ammo!" Bill shouted.

"Take some of mine!" Walter answered throwing him a small cardboard cylinder full of BB's.

"Toby, keep firing and stop them from coming in on us!" shouted Swifty.

"Yes, Sir!" Toby answered as he kept up his rapid pace launching old golf balls, ball bearings, marbles, rocks, sticks and anything he could fit into the sling.

The boys were laughing, shouting orders to each other and, after a chaotic 10-minute battle, all seemed to get quiet, and nothing was heard but the boys' heavy breathing.

Walter stood up to survey the damage, and Toby loaned him his field glasses.

"Cover me I'm going to check for casualties! Hey, what's that white flag?" as he looked through the glasses across the rocky beach and into the opposite woods.

There stood none other than TC waving his white handkerchief while smiling, laughing, and shouting, "I surrender!"

Immediately all the boys came forward and ushered their "prisoner" to the fort for interrogation and laughing while Danny said "I didn't dare come closer while you guys were throwing firecrackers and shooting your guns. Toby almost hit me with a rock, so I backed up to the woods. You guys sure were hitting your targets. If it had been real, I don't think they had a chance to take your position."

Laughing, the boys decided that Danny really wasn't a prisoner but their own "forward observer." They invited him into their fort and gave him a sandwich as thanks for his help. It had been a victorious day!

DIMINISHING PEACE

It was Saturday the 22nd of November before the boys met at the fort again. The weather was 58 degrees and raining, so they were checking the fort's roof for leaks and taking turns cutting up another tire that Toby had found. They all seemed to enjoy these moments when they could talk more as adults.

"My folks can't believe how hot it has been this November," said Bill.

"No one can," added Walter, as he discarded the stripped metal beads from the tire.

Harold Tarbert thought and added, "It is almost like someone is telling us to use the time to get ready for war. "

Swifty asked, "Do you mean another pretend war here or the real thing?"

"No, real war," Harold quickly responded.

Walter piped up, "It's just a matter of time before we join Britain."

"Yeah, ever since Roosevelt signed the Lend-Lease Act last March, we've sent them 50 Destroyers and a lot of war supplies already," added Bill.

"If it reaches them, I hear that German navy and their submarines are sinking a lot of freighters and tankers that are trying to supply the British," inserted Harold.

"They haven't sunk any of our ships, have they?" asked Toby.

"Well, there was a rumor that three or four years ago the Germans sank an American freighter out in the Atlantic off of Narragansett Bay, but no one did anything," Walter answered.

To this Harold added, "No, we haven't seen any American cargo ships sunk, because we put most of our goods on Canadian and British ships. But they did sink one of our destroyers, the USS Reubin James on the 31st of September."

"But our government hasn't made a big thing out of it because we were protecting a convoy and running that risk. We are still technically a neutral nation, but it will all be changing soon, I tell you. We lost a lot of men on the Rubin James," answered Walter.

"And if the Krauts take over Europe, what's to stop them from coming here?" asked Harold.

"We will have to!" asserted Walter. The boys took that as a rallying cry and cheered agreement.

"Bill, what's a submarine? " Tommy asked shyly.

The boys all laughed, but Bill took Tommy's question seriously and made time to explain to Tommy that it was a special ship that could go underwater and sneak up on ships and fire torpedoes at them to sink them.

Tommy look puzzled but, seeing how seriously Bill was answering his question helped.

Walter was the first to chime in to try to help Tom understand by adding,

"A torpedo is like a bomb that has a motor that allows submarines to hide underwater far away from the ship it is trying to sink."

"So they can fire the torpedo and hide so they can't be sunk," added Swifty.

"How do they sink a sub?" asked Toby.

"Ships drop depth charges, which are like time bombs that sink down to the sub before they explode. Planes can bomb them too," added Harold.

Bill said that he had seen a newsreel about the submarine problem during a matinee at the Lyric Theater in Warren. "Sometimes the only thing that gives them away is their periscope, which they can raise above the surface of the water and allow them to look for ships and stay hidden. I hear it takes a keen eye and good binoculars to see them in time to sound an alarm."

Toby inserted, "My dad fought in the Great War, and he hates the Germans and says we should be fighting them now if we want the world to be free. He said that the Germans used submarines and other terrible weapons in the Great War, and they are to be feared."

"FDR should declare war, but he hasn't," added Bill.

"Oh, he's too busy with the Depression to get into a war now," said Swifty.

"Oh Yea, I hear last October Congress made another 'important decision' by declaring the fourth Thursday in November as our National Thanksgiving Day, like ours here in Rhode Island, but he was too busy to sign it," Harold said sarcastically.

"He'll sign it. It makes sense for everyone to celebrate the holiday at the same time," said Swifty.

"Yeah, a National Holiday means no school!!" Toby added.

"As if you need a reason to miss school anyways, Toby," said Bill.

Toby and the boys all laughed.

The rain was letting up, and the fort remained dry, so the boys slowly headed home. Rhode Island's Thanksgiving was approaching, and the warm weather would be staying in the upper 50's, and at night it never would go below freezing. Without the typical snow and winter playing opportunities, Thanksgiving and the coming Christmas holiday period seemed to mean more time with families and less time with friends. Harold announced that he would be heading for London, Ontario to be with relatives over the holiday period. It was the last time they would all be together in such peaceful camaraderie.

FLIGHT TEST

The day after Thanksgiving was a Friday, and Ernie had told the Aero Gang that he wanted them to spend the entire day with him for a special event. They were all there waiting at his shop when he opened the front door at 9:00 a.m. sharp. He made them wait in the front office, escorted them to the back area, and began pulling down the tarpaulin he had used to separate his working area from  the boys' meeting area. As the tarp came down, the boys gasped, for there stood Ernie's 1934 JFDuck, totally restored.

"WOW!!" they all seemed to say in unison

"I thought you guys would like to help me with the finishing touches."

"Gee, it looks pretty done. What more does it need?" Swifty asked.

"Well, I think it could use some yellow paint on the wheel hubs, and the front fairing around the motor should be dark red to help hide the carbon from the exhaust which would really show on the yellow. She also needs a name to be painted on the side. Any ideas?"

The boys quickly went into conference and talked about such famous names as Wiley Post's, Whiney Mae, and Lindberg's Spirit of St. Louis. Anything would be better than Duck which they had been using to refer to as it was being restored. Such alternatives as The Tiverton, Swimming Bird and Magic Wings were being considered when from the back of the gang came Tommy's shy but clear voice saying "2 Ducky 2".

Ernie liked it, saying that it was a second chance for the craft and, after all, it was a Duck. The boys voted, and it was nearly unanimous except with only one 2. 2Ducky was to be painted on both sides of the fuselage, just ahead of the canopy. Ernie announced that D.B. was willing to pencil the script while the boys were painting the cowling red and the wheels yellow. He was going to stencil the plane's identification number, Whiskey 45 Romeo (W45R), in black on the back part of both sides of the fuselage.

At around 12:30, Ernie told the boys to take a break and get clean, because he had ordered some chicken in baskets from the Hummingbird for lunch for everyone. He had no sooner said it when D.B entered carrying the food. Robert Branner jumped up to meet D.B. and hurried to help her ready the tables.

They all enjoyed themselves while D.B. penciled in the name, 2Ducky, on the two sides of the plane. Then, she and Ernie announced that each boy would be given a brush to paint a letter, and the plane would be ready for a test flight over at the Dartmouth airport. As each boy got in line for his brush, several asked, "How are we going to get it there?"

"That's where you guys come in," answered Ernie. "We need to push 2Ducky out of the building, up to that ramp, and onto the trailer, resting her belly on those old tires, tie her down, and haul her up Highland."

"Frank Mortenstein has offered us his pickup for the job. Once we get her in the air and are used to her, and, if all goes well, we will give her a chance at a landing on the bay. Robert will be with me on this flight, as I will be training him to become qualified for seaplane as well as land."

It took the better part of an hour to get the plane diagonally nursed out of the garage door opening to accommodate the wingspan. It was another half hour to get her tied onto the trailer. Once secure, she was hooked on to Mr. Mortenstein's Blue 38 Ford pickup. A typical Ford, it ground its gears and gave its characteristic whine with a telltale trail of smoke as it successfully chugged up Highland and on to the airport.

Oncoming traffic gladly pulled over for the unusual load, and those behind followed in a parade like procession. Many, in fact, followed them right onto the field to watch the strange plane take off. Of course, many of those included every member of the Aero Gang and their families. It was something they had all helped build and definitely something they wouldn't miss seeing. Ernie explained to the crowd that Robert would be with him on this maiden flight to help with the landing gear and get the feel of the plane, as he would be working with Ernie to get his seaplane rating.

"We will start with some touch and go's here on land. Once we are used to her, and, if all goes well, we will leave the pattern and practice landings on water as any Duck is supposed to do."

As Ernie and Robert settled into their seats, Ernie's airport mechanic friends were ready with a ramp to help back the craft off of the trailer. The retractable landing gear protruded about two feet below the flotation hull but, even so, it looked like it was a boat that was going to take off on land. The mechanics also helped Ernie and Robert by giving 2Ducky a second preflight check and were all over the engine. Due to damage from its crash, Ernie had replaced the original Pratt and Whitney R-1830- 62 engine with a Wright R1820Cyclone, giving it 50 more horsepower and about 90 more maximum miles per hour. Indeed, the mechanics had not ever worked on either engine but knew the Wright would give 2Ducky a cruising speed of about 160 mph and a max of around 200.

All were excited to watch her start and warm up for take-off. She did not have a self-starter, so a mechanic had to turn a crank, or windless, to get her to start. Once the RPM's were high enough, Ernie called out, "Clear! Contact!"

2Ducky roared to life in a cloud of oil-rich smoke. Ernie knew it was the oil that was in the cylinders when it was overhauled, but he watched the oil pressure gauge even so. Ernie looked back at

Robert who gave him his characteristic shy grin and an exciting two thumbs up. Ernie gunned the engine and taxied out to the runway, noting the air sock for wind direction. Checking the flaps and rudder, he looked back again at Robert as he slid the canopy closed, pushed in the throttle and started to roll down runway 27, departing on a heading of 270 degrees. The sod runway was far from perfectly level, but, as speed gathered, the tail came up, and Ernie held her down to make sure she was up to speed before beginning her climb. All gauges were right on. More right rudder to compensate for torque steer and, at last, he let her do what she was meant to do...fly. Those watching were mesmerized at the sight. Each one saw their plane get aloft and watched intently as Ernie and Robert took off into the wind, stayed in a pattern, turned left on crosswind, with another left downwind which Ernie extended for quite a while before turning onto the base leg and then a long final.

Ernie did a near perfect touch and go and waggled 2Ducky's wings at the crowd that was waving at them with hats, scarves, gloves, and papers. Robert let out a gurgling laugh of excitement that he couldn't contain. After repeating this procedure twice, Ernie turned downwind again and told Robert to hold on and feel the controls as he maneuvered the plane. Robert knew that Ernie had duplicated all the controls so either pilot could fly, but he was not expecting to be flying on this occasion. Even so, it wasn't long before he was excited to hear Ernie say, "Now, it's your turn, and I will follow you. Remember, stick to the pattern, hold that right rudder in and keep her online for runway 27. You are a little high and fast, bring back the throttle a little more, and try one notch of flaps. Perfect. Now watch her want to land herself. That's it. Pull the nose up, up, up. Great!" Ernie shouted as Robert felt the plane touch the soft sod. "You have just completed one of the toughest touch and go's known, and there are no holes in the hull! Well done, Robert!! Now, do it again."

Robert was relieved as he pushed in the throttle again and brushed the beads of sweat from his brow.

"That was tougher than my first solo," he said out loud.

After a couple more touch and go's for Robert, Ernie said, "Ok now let's head out of the pattern. Try a right departure. Remember to do some clearing turns even if you don't think there is anyone else up here."

2Ducky flew out over Dartmouth and Lincoln Park, and Robert saw the Ferris wheel and rollercoaster. New Bedford and Newport were below, and he saw Mount Hope Bridge and Bristol in the distance as Robert headed for the Warren River. Mr. Blunt, of Blunt Marine, was a friend of Ernie's and a fellow seaplane pilot, and he knew that Ernie would want to show him, 2 Ducky. Ernie turned to look at Robert like he understood what Robert was doing. "I'll take her now, and you keep your hands on the controls as we switch from plane to boat. It is a different feel and takes some getting use to."

The Warren River was an old friend of Ernie's. As a boy, he had fished its waters and brought his catch to the many markets along her shores. It almost seemed like the river was welcoming his return, for it was now at high tide and smooth. 2Ducky calmly set down, and, after a fairly short landing, Ernie taxied her over to the Blunt Marine dock where Danny Cunham, one of Blunt's longshoremen, cast a rope to Robert and helped tie her into her berth. Mr. Blunt was on the dock flashing a grin of excitement at Ernie's accomplishment. The two men exchanged greetings, and, as they walked toward the Blunt Marine office, Robert was introduced and invited in for some refreshment.

As the three men sat in William Blunt's office, Robert cast his eyes around the room to see pictures of planes of WWI and various models on the desk and bookcases. There was a Spad, Sopewith Camel, and a Falker, each done by hand with exceptional detail. Mr. Blunt had been a friend of Ernie's during the war, and the friendship had lasted since. He offered his planes to fly once Robert felt confident in his abilities with 2 Ducky.

"Thank you sir, but I couldn't ......," replied Robert.

"Nonsense!" Blunt interrupted. "You are Ernie's star pupil, and he is the best in my book. If he says you are ready, that is good enough for me!"

"Bill," Ernie said, "I'll call you when he is ready, and you can contact Robert any time afterward to set something up. Robert, you know you said you want to fly everything ever built. You have to start if you ever want to accomplish your goals." The three men laughed, recognizing their own youthful goals to fly anything ever made, at any time, all the time.

The conversation then turned to the world news and the conflicts in Europe and China.

"I'm more concerned about our getting involved in the China thing," stated Ernie.

"Yes, they have been fighting the Japanese since 1931, but because the Chinese fired on them at their Marco Polo Bridge, the Japanese launched a full-scale invasion in 37. Since April, we've had our American Volunteer Group (AVG) helping the Chinese protect Burma with a 100 Curtis-Wright P40's which we were supposed to send to the British. The AVG are called the Flying Tigers, and I guess they are really doing a job on the Japs," Mr. Blunt added.

"I've been reading about them," Robert exclaimed. "Are they wanting volunteers?"

"I suppose they are, but you need more experience in aerobatics first," laughed Ernie.

"It's just a matter of time before we forget about being neutral and declare war!" Blunt exclaimed. "We are a far cry from being ready for a war though," he added.

Ernie thought out loud with a sigh, "It'd take something big to bring us into it. Remember Billy Mitchell's warning about a foreign power hitting us in Hawaii?"

There was a long, thoughtful pause, and they decided to walk back to 2Ducky, get her back to Dartmouth, and look her over for any damage or problems before dark. Mr. Blunt watched enviously as they taxied out on the Warren River and took off.

Noticing the changed air sock as they approached Dartmouth, they entered the pattern downwind for runway 9. 2Ducky settled down gently, and the aero gang dashed over to talk to Ernie and Robert as soon as they shut down.

After a brief walk around the plane and conversations with the gang and friends, Ernie decided to stay with the plane. Robert went home with his family. It had been a pretty full day for all and Robert was ecstatic.

RETURN COMMAND

After picking up Christian, U 87 was a good ways across the Atlantic by November 19th when Captain Bruger received orders from Admiral Donitz, that after resupplying in France, U87 was scheduled to begin her front-line patrol of the North Atlantic on December 1st. Accordingly, Bruger informed his crew that their shore leave would be cut to 48 hours before departure, regretting that his crew would probably have little or no time to be with family before the holiday period. Arriving at her home port of Lubeck, France in the early morning hours of the 23rd, it was obvious that Donitz's orders were being followed. A massive array of shore crews instantly swarmed over the sub, first to inspect and refuel her, and then to resupply her with arms and supplies. Bruger expected his officers to stay with the sub to talk strategy and debriefing concerns from this shakedown cruise. Returning to France was made much quicker by the Gulf Stream current, which provided about six extra knots on the surface and three when submerged. She made it back in nearly record time on the return of her maiden voyage. Donitz's orders were to patrol the New England waters, drop off a team of five saboteurs, and do more invasion surveillance. It was late on the evening of November 25th as the crew staggered back to the sub, resumed their duties and were underway. As ordered, U87 took up her extended North Atlantic patrol west of the coast of Iceland shortly before midnight of December 1st. It was again under the cover of early morning darkness of December 7, 1941, when she resettled into her Sakonnet nest off of Haskins Avenue and reported to Berlin that Talon was again down without incident.

CHEESE AND CRACKERS

It was Sunday, December 7th, and the Branners had returned home from their morning church services at the First Congregational Church in Fall River. The three Branner boys had shed their church clothes in favor of their bib overalls and jeans and were on the living room floor in front of the Philco radio reading the Sunday Boston Herald newspaper. They liked the Boston paper over the Providence Journal because there were more Sunday funny cartoons. Tommy was looking at the funnies, Bill the sports page, and Robert the latest on the war in Europe. Kathryn (Kay) Branner was preparing a roast leg of lamb for their very typical New England Sunday dinner served on or shortly after noon. Dad (William S. Branner) was standing in the open door of the bathroom between the two first floor bedrooms putting away his wooden bowl of Yardley shaving soap, horsehair brush, and Treat razor which he had left on the sink as he had hurriedly readied himself for church. Bill finished the sports page and turned on the Philco to see if he could hear more about sports and the war. Sunday afternoons and evenings offered fun ways for some family time listening to favorite radio shows on the Philco. Jack Benny and his friend, Rochester, always provided some humor for everyone to forget the Depression. President Roosevelt would read the Sunday funnies to the kids because not everyone could afford the luxury of newspapers. Then there were the boys' favorite shows, Straight Arrow, Roy Rogers and Gabby Hayes, Gene Autry, Hopalong Cassidy, The Shadow, and George Burns and Gracie Allen. But the absolute favorite of all the Aero Gang was Sunday's fifteen minute Air Adventures of Jimmy Allen and his sidekick, Speed Robinson. In fact listening to this show is what sparked the enthusiasm of flying in all the boys to some extent as they lived vicariously through Jimmy, the super boy pilot.

This Sunday of leisure was not to be, however. Shortly after Bill turned the Philco on, the voice of John Dailey interrupted the regular broadcast by saying,

"We interrupt this program to inform you that the Japanese have launched a devastating attack on our American Naval Base at Pearl Harbor, Hawaii. Initial reports are limited, but it appears that we have lost many of our ships and many lives."

Bill immediately went to his Dad saying, "The Japanese have bombed Pearl Harbor!"

Mr. Branner, who was now in his bedroom, getting into his golfing clothes for an afternoon round at Newport Country Club, was standing in his undershorts and seemed to freeze as he held onto the hanger with his golfing slacks. He suddenly paled and, being a man who never swore in front of his family, simply exclaimed, "Cheese and Crackers, this means WAR! I'd better head for the plant," as he tended to call the Firestone complex in Fall River. "We have war plans that we need to discuss and implement."

Robert headed for the door saying he was going to get D.B. to drive him to the airport to see if he could learn any more news from the shortwave or hear if the country was going to declare war. Bill said he was going to run over to Ernie's to help him if something came up. Tommy didn't say a word but followed everyone out of the house and headed for the fort where he knew he would find Toby.

"What about my dinner?" Kay asked as she walked beside her husband out to the car.

"It'll keep," her husband answered. "You keep listening to the radio and call me at work if the news changes," her husband shouted while starting his oil burning, blue 34 Ford coup. He waved and headed east on Haskins and disappeared north on 138 towards Fall River.

THINGS MISSING

Just as Tom expected, Toby was in the fort stoking the stove and reading comic books.

"Did ya hear? "Tommy asked

"Hear what?"

"It's bad, Toby!"

"What?"

"War."

"War? Those darn Nazis!"

"No! It's the Japanese!"

"Japanese? But my brother told me that they were fighting China."

"And us now! They bombed Pearl Harbor?"

"Pearl Harbor? Where's that?"

"I don't know, but it was on the radio, and they said we lost a lot of ships and sailors."

"You're sure? It's not just another War of the Worlds scare?"

"No, it's real. My Dad and brothers left before dinner, and they never miss Mom's Sunday dinners."

"We should have some maps so we could look up where we are fighting. I thought we had some maps here, but they are gone. Somebody musta tooked them," Toby stated.

"Yea I heard that lots of stuffs been tooken and people are calling my folks to ask if I tooked em!" Tom exclaimed.

"Mine too. What'd you hear?"

"Well, do you remember my buckets and trowels we use to dig for clams? They're gone!"

"Hum, your right. I heard that Mrs. Hobarth claims she had money taken from her purse a while back," Toby announced.

"Yea and Corrughdo's station across from Joes reported that they had some canned goods stolen," Toby continued.

"My Mom had a pie taken from her cooling shelf she had next to the mudroom window," added Tommy.

Toby continued, "Joe Enfield asked me if I had taken any potatoes and of course ya know who got blamed for all this don't ya?? Yep, good ol Toby Glavin. I don't know why no one believes me."

"Cuz you tell some stories, Toby."

"Yea, but when I'm not laughing, I'm telling the truth, and you know it."

"Yes, I know, but sometimes it is hard to tell, Toby."

"Well, I am really tired of being called a liar and whipped and locked up. It all hurts."

"I'm sorry Toby. I believe you...most times."

"Yea, I know you do. Say, did you see the wires my Dad and I installed in the fort?"

"No," Tommy answered.

"He liked what he saw we had done to the fort, but he didn't like the idea of us using kerosene lanterns for light, so he ran a wire from my house along the stone wall and the trench to the fort. All we need now is a lamp of some sort, and we will have light at night."

"Wow! Wait til the gang sees that!!"

Toby's mood quickly became more buoyant as he felt more like a hero again.

"It's getting late, and I have to go home, Tob," said Tom.

"I'll bet your Mom and Dad are gone."

"How about coming back with a lamp and we can pretend we are at war in our fort and stay overnight?" asked Toby.

"I'll try, but I'll bet my brother has to come too!"

"That's ok."

"Yes, but will he want to?" stated Tom as he slowly trudged up the hill to Ocean View Drive and onto Haskins Avenue and home.

Toby was right. No one was home, so Tommy grabbed a small brass desk lamp from his room, some hot dogs, bread, and milk from the fridge, put it all in a cardboard grocery box, and was just starting to put the box into his wagon when his brother Bill came in after being with Ernie all afternoon.

Tom explained the plan and, since no one was home, Bill decided to leave a note to his parents that they were at the fort for an overnight. Tom was excited and ran to get some blankets and pillows. Bill secured the grocery box and some newspapers for the sandy floor of the fort to the wagon and followed Tommy out the door and down the street.

Toby's stove fire had the fort a little too warm, so he was sitting outside when Bill and Tom Branner showed up. December had started out like November and was unusually warm. In fact, they had not yet had even one night that went below freezing. Still, it was nice to have the stove to take the chill off when the gang got together.

Bill put the newspapers on the earthen floor to serve as a liner from the cold and dampness and then placed the blankets and pillows on top. Toby and Tommy followed, and the three began boiling some hot dogs for supper. Smiling, Toby pulled out three 8 oz bottles of Grape Nehi and some cookies he had brought from home.

Bill didn't always like to admit it but, even at 15, he liked to "rough it" or camp out and found that he missed times like this. He wished that this life could continue, but the thought of war was still on his mind, and he knew that there were some big changes coming. Tommy pulled out the lamp he brought and, as dusk settled, the boys enjoyed both the warmth and glow of the stove and the convenience of the one light bulb.

"Wonder if we will declare war tonight or tomorrow," Bill said out loud. Toby and Tommy did not answer and just looked at him unknowingly.

Did you guys just hear something outside? Tommy asked

"No," Bill replied. "What did it sound like?"

"A splash," Tommy answered.

"Probably just a fish jumping," Toby stated.

Bill grabbed one of the fort's silver and black Eveready flashlights and stepped outside to shine it in the direction of the river.

"I didn't see anything," Bill said as he soon returned to the fort. Want to play checkers or read comics?"

"I haven't finished the Shadow comic!" said Toby as Tommy grabbed his favorite Superman story, and Bill picked up his Popular Aviation magazine. They all were quietly reading but before long were asleep on their cozy makeshift bed.

SHOCKED SURPRISE

Captain Bruger could tell that Christian was bothered about something as he entered the captain's quarters following his recent meeting with his onshore contacts. Before he could say anything Christian was first to speak.

"Have you had any messages from Berlin? "He asked.

"No, why?"

"Everyone is talking about Pearl Harbor being attacked by the Japanese!"

"NO! IT CANNOT BE! "Exclaimed the shocked captain. "Berlin said the Japanese told us they wouldn't act until we coordinated with them. We need at least a year before we can invade!"

Bruger continued as he stood up from his desk. "I need to go to the radio room and communicate with Berlin for confirmation," he added as he stepped out the doorway.

Christian remained quietly reflecting in the captain's quarters as Wallie Jung, and Albert Schneppit entered. They immediately began questioning Christian about what he had observed in his last "outing," obviously jealous that Christian could come and go while they had to stay with U87. Christian calmly replied, "I report to only the captain."

Wachoffizer Jung's face reddened and loudly admonished Christian with a bold statement, "I am the second in command, and I am ordering you to tell me what you observed."

As he talked, Schneppit (Specks) leaned his body into Christian and pinned Christian's arms against the bulkhead wall. Christian immediately brought his knee up and into Streit's groin and chopped his arms away, readying for Speck's next move. Jung quickly stepped in between the two men and quietly threatened again that it would be in Christian's best interest to comply with a

80

commanding officers request. The later comments were overheard and partly observed by Captain Bruger who reentered his quarters quickly and dismissed both aggressors, despite their obvious objecting affect.

Once they had left, Captain Bruger addressed Christian,

"You had better watch yourself with those two. I have my reasons to just tell them enough and no more. They could be dangerous."

"I understand, my Captain," replied Christian with a sly smile "Did Berlin confirm?"

"Ja, that that they did, and, it is like I expected, the Führer and high command is very upset with the Japanese deciding to ignore our input and act on their own. It may just jeopardize the Axis agreement. We really need them to divide America's attention and fight a two frontal war, if we are to succeed."

There was a long pause, and then Bruger added, "Strange though, Admiral Donitz seemed to be rejoicing and claiming that this opportunity will open up lots of action for our U-boats off the American Atlantic coast."

I imagine that Hitler will declare war against America now," stated Christian.

"It is a matter of days, added Bruger, "We had better make contact with our men ashore and fill them in on our plans. What is your estimate of the least amount of time you will need to make contact ashore again?"

"Three days, sir."

"The 11th then."

"Yes, sir. I shall target noon our time to be back here so we can depart."

"That's good. The tide will be coming in, and we will need it to sail quickly without the cover of darkness. We may be at war by then."

"Yes, but the Americans are not ready around here," Christian asserted

DAY OF INFAMY

It was December 8th, and everyone gathered in the homes of anyone who had a radio to hear President Roosevelt deliver his speech and ask Congress to formally declare war on the Japanese. Many neighbors came into the Branner's living room to listen to their Philco. Following the speech and newscaster commentary, there were advisories about what citizens could do to help the war effort. The east coast needed to worry about the possibility of air raids and naval bombardment, so it was recommended that everyone put up blackout curtains to minimize targeting by the enemy. Headlights on autos were to be painted black except for tiny slits to minimize lighting. Citizens were told to conserve on gasoline, and before long there would be A, B, and C ration I.D. stickers issued for application onto all windshields of automobiles and trucks. Almost overnight food, medical supplies, and consumer goods were in short supply so we could amass such things for our soldiers and sailors. Families were torn as brothers and fathers enlisted, and everyone did their part for the cause. December 11th came, and once again radios and newspapers announced that Germany had declared war on the United States. It was indeed a World War, and the United States was no longer neutral.

Whenever Toby and Tommy were bothered about what the adults were saying it was good to have a place like the fort to go to. Toby was already there when Tommy arrived.

"Gosh," Tommy said, "My mom is really upset and crying and all about the war."

"I know, so's mine."

"Do ya think it will come here?"

"What?" Toby asked

"The War!"

"I don't know, but we need to be ready. I don't even own a gun."

"We don't either. But if they come, I'll bet my dad and brother will know where to get em," Tommy said defiantly.

"But if they come, we can make it tough for them by poisoning them, burning the land, and putting sand and sugar in their gas tanks."

"What does that do?"

"My dad says that it messes up engines and they can't run."

"Wow, Toby you know a lot."

"Yea but you are the only one who knows that, besides me!" Toby chuckled. "I know one other thing. We are low on fish at our house, and my mom asked me to put the raft in and try to catch something. Kind of hard without worms or minnows this time of year, but my dad and brother and I made some lures to try."

"Good luck Toby! I'll cut up some more tires and gather more driftwood while you are out there."

Toby slid his raft into the water and jumped in while it was sliding over the edge of the shore. Even though it was warm for December, there was a cool breeze, and it was never good to get any part of you wet. Toby was also dressed warm with his new matching checkered red and black wool hunters' jacket and earflap cap. He liked the outfit because it made him look bigger and older than he was.

Successful at getting in the raft without getting wet, Toby was also glad that he had used his tar patch goo to seal his leaks on the raft's bottom. Just to be on the safe side, he always made sure he had his little rubber cement can of it with him when he went out to fish. The stuff was easy to spread with the brush that was part of the lid, even when the surface was cold and wet. He kept it in the long side pouch next to his homemade spear, harpoon, fishing rod, hunting knife, and pliers. That way he was ready for any kind of fish, large or small.

Toby waved to Tommy who was on the shore picking up some driftwood for the fort. Tommy waved back and watched Toby as he paddled toward an object in the water. Although it came to the surface next to Toby's raft, it appeared to be looking away from him. The object appeared to be following a fast-moving Navy Shore Patrol Boat that routinely cruised the Sakonnet twice a day.

As the object started to turn, Toby quickly paddled to stay behind the sweep of the object, so it did not look at him. "Oh, Boogers! I bet I'm going to get in trouble again!" he said out loud as he kept trying to stay behind the lens at all times.

"So you all don't believe me, huh," he again said out loud. "Well, you bloody buggers, not this time!"

Toby pulled out his sealant can and, reaching around from behind the periscope, began to paint the lens with the black, sticky, goo.

Down in U87 Watch Commander, Wallie Jung was at the periscope commencing a procedural safety sweep prior to surfacing and focused on the Navy Patrol Boat. In such a restricted area, he knew that there was nothing toward shore, but he had to make sure that there was no navy or commercial traffic to contend with as they surfaced. He was startled when he caught a brief glimpse of a hand painting his vision black. Swearing in German, he ordered the periscope down and sent Specks to go to the surface and eliminate the problem.

It didn't take long before there was a man on the surface swimming toward Toby's raft. Toby was expecting something to happen as soon as the periscope disappeared and frantically shouted to Tommy to go for help while he pulled out his spear and harpoon to fend the man off and stop him from climbing onto his life raft. As Tom started to run, he saw another man come out of the woods and jump into the water in the direction of Toby's raft. He recognized the man as Christian but couldn't remember his name. As Tommy ran, he turned to look back from the wall and was scared to see that there was a big boat rising up behind Toby's raft. He knew Toby was in big trouble and ran as fast as he could to try to get help. Gasping for air, he stormed into Glavin's kitchen and screamed for help. There was no answer. Not willing to wait, he bolted up the road to Haskins and saw D.B. backing her Studebaker out of her parking space and turning to go toward town. Tommy tripped and banged his hand on her car as he ran with all his might. He screamed, and D.B. hit her brakes and jumped out thinking she had run over Tommy. She helped him up, but he quickly jumped into her Studebaker and screamed,

"GET JOE!"

Sensing it was serious, she quickly complied, and they roared down to Joe's Shack. Joe was organizing his supply shelves when he heard DB rapidly pull up and lock her brakes to a skidding stop. Without giving him time to say hi, Tommy jumped out and screamed, "Toby, raft, submarine!"

Not really knowing what was up, Joe knew Tommy well enough to know that Toby was in trouble again, and with Tommy pointing to the Enfield in the corner, he didn't hesitate to grab it and a box of shells, put up his "Closed" sign and use his crutch to vault to D.B.'s Studebaker.

`Tommy had calmed down a little enough to explain that some men were after Toby in his raft, and there was a ship of some sort, possibly a submarine.

D.B. broke the land speed record for the half-mile to Toby's house and drove across the lawn to the back wall where Joe jumped out and hobbled for the trench, using his crutch and his Enfield to support him.

D.B. could see the sub and raft and quickly turned around and headed for the airport to tell Robert and anyone she thought could do something. She and Tommy headed back up Haskins Avenue and saw Tommy's brother, Bill, walking down their driveway, probably heading for Ernie's as he did almost every day. D.B. stopped, shouting, "Get in!!!" and explained the situation as best she could. Bill took it all in and said, "Let me off at Ernie's, and I will see if he has any ideas." D.B. quickly nodded in agreement.

IN POSITION

In spite of his disability, Joe had been down to the fort on several occasions and had little trouble quickly navigating the trench to the fort and the far right trench that Toby had dug himself. Besides, he still remembered a lot about the war in the trenches, and he was soon settled in position and looked out toward the voices he knew were German. Then he gasped as he saw the submarine! There were few markings on it, but the sail of the conning tower had what looked like a sinister, giant, eagle talon painted on it. There were two more men coming out of the sub and calling, in German, for the men in the water to return.

The two blond men in the water were Albert Schneppit (Specs) and Christian Dieterman with Specs trying to board and hurt Toby with a knife. That was all Joe needed to see, and he was now in a position to do something to save Toby. Joe knew his Enfield was very accurate to 200 yards and figured the distance was a little less. He put a bead on the man trying to get onto the raft and held it on him. The other man was the "fisherman" who occasionally stopped by his stand; the one who called himself Christian. Joe thought it ironic for a Nazi to be called Christian and mentally changed his name to Donkey, as he continued to hold his bead on the first man. Donkey Christian was now swimming close behind and shouting, "Nein! Nein!". A third man with dark hair was not saying anything but swimming strongly toward the raft but further away. Toby was standing with his legs spread wide and crouched over with his makeshift spear poking at the first man, trying to stop him from getting on the raft. The man swung his arm out, grabbed the spear, and pulled it from Toby's grasp. Toby then reached for his harpoon, caught Specs forearm with one of the prongs, and it did not come back out. At this point, Toby pulled out his rather small hunting knife ready for the man to go after him. The man started to climb aboard and paused to pull out a huge bayonet-like knife.

"Oh, boogers!" Toby exclaimed as he stared at the size of the knife. Specs swung violently and cut off the handle of the harpoon with one swift chop, leaving the prong still in his arm. Toby exclaimed, "No!!!" as the man climbed onto the raft and turned to Toby, advancing with the huge knife. Toby backed up but realized he had no more room as the man raised his weapon. The man suddenly paused as if he was thinking, and Toby heard the first report of Joe's Enfield. A small hole appeared in the center of the man's forehead followed by an instant explosion of the man's head. After another report, there was red splatter in the raft as he fell back into the water. He landed next to Georg Kurtzman, who quickly cradled the man's body and asked Christian to help get him back to the sub. Turning toward Toby, Christian said, "Take care, Toby. Go with God."

Toby simply stared at the men, and in a primal voice from deep within his heavy breaths, he shouted, "You bloody boogers, go to hell, Nazis," repeating the oath several times as he paddled feverishly toward the fort and the safety of Joe's arms.

Christian and George floated Specs body back to the sub, as it hurriedly prepared to head for open waters.

Meanwhile, Bill Branner dashed to the back of Ernie's shop calling his name. Ernie waved from way down the back alley as he was walking back from the wharf where the Balboa Oil Company was allowing him to dock 2Ducky. Bill ran to Ernie and explained about the sub as best he could. Ernie and Bill turned and sprinted back to 2 Ducky. Bill ran to the rope tie downs and untied them as Ernie turned the crank and tried to fire off 2 Ducky by himself, unsuccessfully. He then called to Bill to turn the starter crank and jumped into the cockpit and fired off the engine. Bill jumped down and undid the last tie down, and Ernie began taxiing out onto the river, checking that the wind direction was from the northwest and immediately went to full throttle, lifted 2 Ducky up to about 20 feet above the surface, and held her steady. In short order, he saw the sub which was heading toward him. Ernie kept 2Ducky low and headed right for the sub's antennas. He saw what he thought was the captain pointing at him and a man on the deck shooting some type of machine gun. Ernie could hear the slugs tearing through the fabric of the 2Ducky's hull. But he kept her low and took out the sub's antennas. He immediately climbed to about 100 ft. and circled to the left, coming about for a starboard attack with no armament.

Ernie thought, "If I can scare them to maneuver into the shallows, she might run aground and give our navy time to come in for a kill."

Then he felt a sudden lurch as 2 Ducky was hit by the sub's flack gun and something heavy passed through the fuselage behind him. Ernie decided to limp to the Dartmouth airport rather than continuing his attacks or chance a landing on water and sinking. 2Ducky was harder to control, but in spite of her damage, she got Ernie over Dartmouth field and lined up for a landing. He brought her in and taxied up to the ground crew that was just seeing another plane off. He saw that it was Robert in his Wasp but had no time to flag him down.

THE WASP

After dropping Bill off at Ernie's, D.B. didn't waste any time getting her Studebaker up Highland and over to Dartmouth in record time. At the airport, she drove right up to the hangers and laid on her horn until the mechanics came out. She then took command and informed them that there was a German sub in the Sakonnet River heading for open water. She said that she thought Ernie and William were trying to slow the sub's exit by buzzing it with 2 Ducky. She asked if they could get Robert's plane ready to help Ernie slow the sub down while she called the Newport Naval Air Station from the airport phone. To everyone's surprise, she grabbed Robert by the shoulders and gave him a big hug and kissed him right on the mouth.

"You will do it, Rob, won't you?"

"Darn right, I will!" Robert answered with a surprised smile on his face. "I've been dreaming of a moment like this!" not too sure if he meant the kiss or the mission.

"You will do fine. I am proud of you, Rob! Now, I have to get through to the Navy, if someone hasn't already. You get going and make them pay!" She then turned and walked toward the office to make her call. Robert paused a quick moment to watch her walk away, and then he took a few strides and jumped up the side and into his Wasp as he called it. It had a Pratt &Whitney R1340 (Wasp) engine and kind of looked like a wasp with its yellow wings and tail and black and red fuselage.

Danny saw Robert board the Wasp and came running over before Robert started up and said that he had to come along adding, "You have no armament. How are you going to stop a sub?"

"I intend to slow it down or get it to beach."

"What if I told you I made a bomb?"

If anyone else had made such a statement, it is doubtful Robert would have believed it. But, this was Danny, and Robert instantly knew that since Danny was always experimenting and trying anything, he just gave Danny a broad grin and said, "Then, let's give 'er a try, Danny!"

Dan ran back to the hanger and came running out with a five-gallon tar drum wrapped in oil-soaked burlap, with a tow chain attached to a reinforced handle. "That's a bomb?" exclaimed Robert shaking his head.

"Don't doubt me!" Dan retorted as he attached the tow chain to the fixed landing gear and swung the tar bucket into the second seat while climbing in at the same time. The mechanics now had the Wasp gassed and ready to go and were cranking the starter.

"Robert yelled, "Clear," and the Wasp roared to life in a large blue cloud of smoke.

As they taxied down the runway, Danny stood up and shouted to Robert,

"You take her in low, and I will light this thing and throw it over. It has to crash into the sub and bust open to blow, but I've added some gasoline and kerosene and soap to it, so it should light off, spread, and stick to whatever it hits. It just may be enough to scare them to death!" he said laughing. "If you can, aim for their crew, as they will be sure to be shooting at us. It will be just like when we go bowling, only this time you better get a strike or as many "pins" as you can! No time for gutter balls!!!"

"Always a joker!" Robert shouted back to Danny as he pushed in the throttle and headed for straight out departure on 27.

While they were heading out, Danny was holding the tar bomb in his lap and trying to figure out how to make his Zippo Lighter work in the wind. He decided to use the visor of his Red Sox baseball cap as a windbreak while he struck the lighter. Once the oil-soaked burlap ignited, it probably would stay lit as he lowered it over the side. He had his face covered with a scarf and had his leather jacket and extra long shop gloves for flame protection, so he felt confident his idea would work.

At 90 miles an hour, it was only about six minutes of airtime before they saw the sub. Ernie had made it leave the channel, so it was in the shallower shoal area of the river just before the Balboa Oil pipeline. The tide was not fully up yet, so Robert decided to try to blindside the sub by coming in low over the town of Tiverton and drop down from the cliff side. That would give them a little more than a quarter mile to drop 100 feet and smash the boat with the tar bomb. Danny understood what Robert was thinking and planned to light the burlap just as they passed over the cliff. With luck, the speed of the plane would hold the bomb out at the same level as the landing gear some 50 feet beyond the tail. On contact with the sub, the container should burst open in a sticky ball of fire. The chain and damaged barrel would stay connected to the gear and, if Robert wanted to, he could use it again like a medieval mace to club the sub with each extra pass. It should be enough to keep the Germans away from their guns and continue to delay them until the Navy came.

"Here we go!" said Robert as they skimmed over the telephone poles along highway 138 and banked over what looked like Haskins Avenue. Crabbing to the left, they passed over the Balboa tanks. Danny lit his Zippo. The extra large flame from the Zippo caught the burlap almost immediately, and Robert looked back to see Danny pushing the ball of flame over the side and playing out the chain. Danny kept his eyes on the barrel and gave Robert thumbs up. Robert took the Wasp in low with the throttle wide open.

The German crew had been fooled, as they were all looking out to the open water and not toward the land. Suddenly they heard the Wasp's engine and turned to see the plane on top of them with the dangling tar bomb heading right for them. The bomb hit U87 to the right side of the sail tower, and, instantly, there was a wall of flame that hit the sail, deck gun, and a few of the crew. The sub seemed to turn to starboard and move further into the sandy shoal. Danny let out a yell. "We did it, Robert! I think she's gone aground! Careful now, they are going to be really mad!!"

Robert was banking for a return pass and working to use the chain to rake the sub's deck and keep the crew from the deck gun. He was successful with the second pass as well and knocked two Germans into the water. He wasn't expecting such accuracy from their small arms fire, and as he came in on his third pass, he suddenly felt the Wasp take a hit and the engine just stopped. Without power, he tried to pull a series of lifts to get closer to shore, but that only pulled her up and into a stall that dropped her like a rock and pancaked her into the shore. The impact threw Danny clear and into deeper water, but Robert was still strapped in and trapped by the plane's debris in the muddy shore water.

Walter Peel and his dad had been fishing in his rowboat, spellbound as he saw his friend buzzing the sub. Walter quickly rowed toward Danny who said he was ok and told him to get Robert. Walter dove in and unfastened Robert's harness and pulled him to the surface and onto his rowboat. Danny climbed in, and the two took turns pressing on Robert's chest to try to get the muddy water out of his lungs, while Mr. Peel rowed to shore. Robert was unconscious and turning a bluish color. As Danny continued compressing Robert's chest, Mr. Peel and Walter hurriedly got Robert and Danny to their car for a ride to The Truesdale Hospital in Fall River.

NO WAY!

D. B. was becoming very frustrated that no one at the Newport Naval Air Station would listen to her report of a German sub in the Sakonnet River/ Mt. Hope bay area. The man on the other end of the line thought it sounded like a prank caller and said that it would be too soon for German forces to be in the area when they just declared war this morning, and there had been no sightings by American planes or the 243rd Regiment of the Coastal Defense System.

"There is just no way there could be a sub in our waters, mam!"

"Listen to me, I saw the sub, darn you!" she insisted. "I need to talk to someone in authority who will at least authorize a fly over to verify my report. We have civilians trying to delay the sub, so you have time to get to it somehow. Every minute you delay by putting me off is a victory for Germany, you fool."

"Just a minute and I will try to connect you to our C.O.," the man said reluctantly. There was a long pause, and then the phone went dead.

"Oh, for the love of Pete!" she blurted, dialing again for the umpteenth time. "I'm not giving up that easily," she said aloud as her brown eyes flashed with angry disgust.

"Sir, this lady keeps calling and is insisting that she talk to you about an enemy sub in the Sakonnet River. I've told her that we had no confirmation of any enemy activity in our area, but she won't take no for an answer."

"Put her on, ensign."

"Yes, Sir!"

This is Captain Gifford"

"Gordon Gifford?" D.B. asked, recognizing the name of a former acquaintance.

"This is D. B. I have been trying to get through to someone. Perhaps, since you may remember me and know I am not crazy, you will listen."

"Go ahead, D.B. How are you?"

"I'm fine, but a bit ticked off that no one will listen to me. Captain, there is an enemy submarine in our waters, and we have two civilian planes trying to get the sub to slow its escape to deep water. Please send a plane or someone to intercept the sub."

"D.B., I don't doubt your sincerity, but this day has everyone playing war, and our phones are ringing off their hooks with false reports of enemy soldiers and blimps and ships. As we check them out, they are all false. Most of them are our ships or nothing."

D.B. curtly interrupted by saying, "CAPTAIN GIFFORD, I AM NOT A QUACK BUT YOU SIR ARE A NUMBSKULL!!"

A bit taken back by her assertiveness, the captain continued, "I'll tell you what. I will leave personal word for the next observation plane to take a look at the Sakonnet River area, and I'll even notify the PT Squadron that trains in the Mt. Hope Bay near Spar Island. They will be the closest if our spotter sees something. I can't imagine that any sub could navigate that river, and besides the 243rd Army regiment is actively deploying a 1200 man Coastal Defense Battery with 12 inch guns, anti-aircraft, and 50 caliber machine guns, while we are laying an active minefield consisting of 8 groups of mines, and anti-submarine barriers across Mt. Hope and Narragansett Bays, leaving only 11,000 yards of open channel. The Sakonnet is not navigable. It is doubtful that this boat you are talking about has not been seen, but I can assure you we'll check into it, just like we are checking into the other reports."

"YES, I know all that. Cut the B.S., will you? You are just wasting time with talk. Can you put a priority on my report?"

"I will try, but I am only a captain of one unit, and I cannot order other units. But again, I WILL TRY. Thank you for your report. Perhaps we can talk again soon, at a less strenuous time."

"Perhaps," she answered weakly and hung up. "Fat chance of that, Gord ON!!!" she muttered angrily. She slowly walked out of the airport office and toward her car which she affectionately called Baker, and sat in the driver's seat.

"Well Baker, we did it," she said in an exhausted voice. "Now we just need to wait till Robert and Danny return." As she sat in her car, she saw Ernie hurriedly climb into another plane, start, and take off toward the Sakonnet. She knew that he was going back to help Robert, somehow.

FURIOUS!

Captain Bruger was furious with the actions of his crew. "Who authorized you to leave this boat?" he demanded of Georg Kurtzman.

"Wallie Jung told me to go after Specks before he did something stupid," Kurtzman answered.

Bruger's blood was boiling as he spat out his venom, "Enough about Schneppit! He's dead. How? I don't know, but we have much bigger problems. You get up top and see if you can clean that gunk off the periscope." Over the phone, he talked to Dieter Wilhelm, his engineer, and told him to blow all ballast, move all crew and items of extra weight aft, and continue to keep trying to back the sub out of the sands with the rising tide.

"Christian, why were you involved in this?"

"I was returning from meeting with our contacts as ordered and saw what was unfolding. I didn't want Specks to hurt the boy, sir, and I knew he was delaying our departure. I'm sorry I wasn't here to counter the orders of Jung," he continued.

"And I am sorry that I was in my quarters, trusting the command to my subordinates while I worked on our patrol plans for the open waters!" Bruger steamed. "Now we have to sit here like ducks and hope that the Americans continue to send us unarmed planes. Otherwise, all is lost. We need to ignore the planes and help get this sub into the channel so we can get back to doing what we were ordered to do!

As the captain talked, everyone felt U87 shudder and slide backward. Bruger quickly dashed topside to direct his boat into the channel just as another plane buzzed by. "Damn those little yellow and red planes! They aren't hurting us, but they sure could draw a lot of attention our way. Let's get going!" He then ordered his crew to take axes and quickly chop through the floating rubber Balboa oil supply pipeline so U87 could slip to the mouth of the Sakonnet and out into the bay all the while being circled by Ernie's one lone aircraft.

Finally, Bruger's sonar showed enough depth available to start to submerge into Rhode Island Sound. A few moments later, the crew heard the sound of distant explosions from depth charges dropped from U.S. Navy planes that had arrived too late, and with obviously no idea of the sub's exact location, to do any damage.

Ernie had tried to stay with the sub as long as he could, but once it submerged it was soon lost to the depths and its evasive maneuvers. He continued to expand his circle out over the Atlantic when the Navy planes arrived and dropped their depth charges.

"Too little too late!" he thought to himself and turned his craft back toward Dartmouth. As he flew up the Sakonnet, he saw the wreckage of the Wasp and knew it was bad for Robert and Danny. After landing, it was Ernie who informed D.B. that Robert and Danny had crashed. He quickly went to the phone and called his shop in hopes that someone would answer. Finally, Walter Peel picked up the phone.

"Ernie! Oh, am I glad it is you! It's awful. Robert and Danny are on their way to Trusdale, and Robert looked dead. Danny was ok as far as I can tell. Bill is still here but is heading home to tell his mom."

"Tell him that D.B. will pick him and his mom up and take them to the hospital. I'll try to reach his dad at Firestone and take him over. Tommy will probably be with Toby, and they both know to go to Mc Ardel's, but Bill can remind them if they are home already."

"Ok, Ernie. I'll stay here till you get back."

"Thanks, Walter!!!" You've done well!

TRUSDALE

The reception area of Trusdale Hospital was Spartan, to say the least. A cold, damp air joined in with the bland, white walls, and grey, cement floors of the emergency room entrance and made it hard to enjoy being in this life-saving institution. But there was a war on, and the reality of things was that there were others who had it worse and civilians had to do with less so our soldiers and sailors could have the medications and care they needed. Everyone seemed to accept their plight without complaining.

Dr. Konig stood in the lobby waiting for everyone as Ernie Gibson escorted William Branner past the admission desk to join his wife, Kathryn, and son, Bill, in the empty lobby.

Dr. Konig wasted no time to report Robert's status. The accident had caused Robert to ingest and inhale a lot of shore water, and he had quickly developed allergic lesions on his lungs, skin, and in his internal organs that had the doctors very concerned. Robert was experiencing a lot of pain from the hemorrhaging of the lesions. He would need a lot of O+ blood transfusions from anyone with the same blood type.

Dr. Konig had already consulted with a Dr. Galene, Director of Surgery, regarding Robert's condition and decided that surgery was not called for at this time. Instead, the two doctors felt that, since Robert was not yet 18, he might have a more comprehensive allergy, infection, and blood consultation at the Boston Children's Hospital. If the Branners would agree, Dr. Konig would immediately refer Robert to Boston as soon as he was stable enough to endure the 50+ mile car ride.

The Branners readily agreed and signed the necessary referral papers. They all felt that it was fortunate that Robert was still considered a minor.

"It won't be easy." Dr. Konig added. "With the War, medications will be scarce, and you will have to beg or borrow gas rations to go to visit. His condition is such that I don't think he will be coming home anytime soon."

"We understand, Doctor," Mr. Branner replied. "You mentioned that Robert needs O+ blood. That's my type." Dr. Konig simply stated, "Follow me. Robert will probably need another transfusion yet tonight. He should be stable for transport tomorrow. Will you be able to take him?"

"Certainly," Kathryn replied.

HOME AGAIN

It was late in the evening when Kathryn and Bill Branner returned from the hospital, and they were surprised to find the lights on and some strange cars in the driveway. When they entered their house, they were greeted by Bill and Tommy who mentioned that there were some Navy men who wanted to talk to them.

"Hello, Mr. and Mrs. Branner. Your boys have been good hosts and invited us in to wait for your return. How is Robert doing?"

"As well as can be expected, I guess," answered Mr. Branner.

"My name is Commander Jacobs, and I am sorry to impose on you at this hour after such a trying day. However, it is urgent that we know if you informed anyone at the hospital as to how Robert was injured?"

"No," answered Kathryn. "All we know is that his plane crashed."

Jacobs answered, "That is fortunate because we feel that it is important that we only recognize that fact. We have been conducting maneuvers in the Bay area to see how well we respond to possible enemy infiltration, and in the interest of national security we need to keep the nature of these maneuvers very quiet, or the local population might panic. That could be very damaging to the nation's morale."

"So what happened?" asked Mrs. Branner.

"Well, it appears that for some reason Robert and another pilot, a Mr. Gibson, I believe, attacked a submarine and since we are at war, they were fired on. Both planes were hit, but Robert's was downed, and he crash landed on the shore and was rescued by Walter Peel and his dad. Mr. Gibson nursed his craft and landed at Dartmouth. The local people who helped Robert saw no submarine. So that leaves Peel and his dad, Danny Lopez, Tommy, Toby Glavin, Joe Foraro and Dorothy Burgett, in addition to

Robert and Gibson, who actually saw the sub. We have explained everything to everyone involved and got them to promise to not divulge the actual incident to the press or anyone who inquires or asks for details. Early tomorrow morning you all will be picked up and transported to the Newport Naval War College for a meeting with representatives from the Navy, War Department, Secret Service, and the office of the President. I expect your ride will be here by 8:00 a.m. and, if all goes as planned, you should be back by noon. Do any of you have any questions?"

The silence was broken by Toby Glavin. "It wasn't our submarine. It had a claw talon on its tower. The guy spoke German and had a knife. He was going to kill me. Joe shot him," Toby explained.

Commander Jacobs froze. He knew of no close contact with an enemy combatant or armed conflict, or of any casualties. Without drawing attention to this revelation, he calmly continued, "We will investigate your claim and have some answers for you in the morning. Can you all be available?"

All agreed although Toby said he had to ask his mom first.

Commander Jacobs smiled and told Toby that she and his dad would be coming along.

TO "COLLEGE"

The main building of the campus of the War College was a three-story sandstone cube-like structure built in the late 1800's but kept spotlessly. The grey Navy Chevrolet cars carrying the Aero Gang members and their families arrived in timely precision, converging on the entrance at the same time and one by one clearing the security booth manned by Shore Police (SP) officers in khaki uniforms with white helmets. They all entered the building at the same time and were led to a large room where there was a huge floor, relief map of the world occupying approximately 80% of the room's floor space. On the map were toy-like ships that could be moved by sailors with long shuffleboard like poles. Danny Lopez was surprised to see his uncle John was one of the men moving the ships around the board and inconspicuously waved to him as John winked back.

Commander Jacobs met the group by the map and explained that the board was always kept up to date as to the location of U.S. and allied navy ships and any possible enemy fleets that were detected. It did not take a military strategist to see that most of the American and allied fleets were far away from the U.S.A. and, for now, America had to rely on the Coast Guard and volunteers to protect her waters. Surprisingly, there was no sign of any U-boats off the east coast shores, and Danny asked why?

Commander Jacobs answered, "Our intelligence tells us that the Germans only have four subs in the Atlantic presently and only two are active. We suspect the other two are for weather forecasting. We know that they are presently strengthening their forces and constructing submarines in Germany and France. The British are making every effort to bomb German shipbuilding facilities when they can. We know that the Nazis plan to step up their sub attacks on our convoys to Britain in the near future, but we have no reports of any activity in our area. Would you all please follow me into the adjoining room?"

The group went through three doors that were each guarded by two Marines at attention with rifles and bayonets. Suddenly everyone in the group was keenly aware that things were serious.

As they entered the room, they were asked to be seated in the wooden folding chairs that had been set up audience style facing a large conference table which had some very official persons already seated. Although none of the Navy and Secret Service people were familiar to anyone, Mr. Branner recognized the man in the middle as President Roosevelt's personal representative and whispered to Kathryn and Billy, "That's Roosevelt's Under Secretary of State, Sumner Wells."

This English looking, mustached man was dressed in a pinstriped suit with a matching vest, white shirt, and dark blue bow tie. He seemed a confident leader and commanded a considerable amount of respect from the rest of the panel members. He opened the meeting by welcoming all present and thanking them for being prompt.

"All of us present know what actually happened yesterday, but we have, we feel, been successful at not causing panic with the rest of the citizens of Tiverton and our nation. President Roosevelt has asked me to convey that it would be most unfortunate to let anyone, especially the press, think that we had been invaded here on the east coast so early in the war. I am certain that you older folks understand this. It is with you young people that we have some concern. Do you understand the seriousness of what I am saying? We cannot tell anyone anything about Robert crashing as a result of German submarine gunfire. If you do, we will have no recourse but to call you a liar and see to it that you are locked away so as to not talk to anyone and cause panic and poor moral around New England."

His words seemed to sink into everyone's mind, and the rest of the conversations were just formalities. The group was excused and provided very quiet transportation back home. Indeed, no one spoke until the Branners, and the Glavins were sitting in the Branners' parlor. Mr. Glavin looked at Toby with apologetic eyes as Toby exclaimed! "It ain't right!"

"What do you mean?" asked Mr. Branner.

"It ain't right that we are being told by our government to not tell what happened. Our government is supposed to be a good government, and they are telling us to lie.

"That's right, Toby," answered Mr. Branner. "We are at war, and this is what we need to do to help us fight the war. To do otherwise would be helping the enemy. We all were shocked at Pearl Harbor and the Philippine invasions. Our nation might lose its willingness to fight if we are told that we might be invaded soon," he concluded.

"Do you understand Toby?" asked his father.

"I guess so. It ain't right, but I will be quiet until the war is over."

Mr. Branner took the edge off by saying, "That's the stuff, Toby! In the meantime, everyone needs to pull together for the war, and I know you boys can help our Lions Club and Boy Scouts collect for a huge scrap drive later this month. Care to help?"

The boys nodded that they would.

"We need to know who has paper, metal, wood, and rubber materials that can be used again. They need to be informed of the drive and help gather and load our trucks. Bill, your Mom and I will be traveling to Boston a lot to see Rob. So, I'm putting you in charge to get your Aero Gang involved. Can you do this?"

"If it will help Robert and our country, I know the gang will gladly lend a hand, Dad," Bill answered.

SCRAP DRIVE

The next few days were a blur, and it was now the 14th of December. Although colder at night, the days continued to be unusually warm, and the Aero Gang was excited about riding in the trucks to inform people of the actual drive on the 28th. As promised, Bill divided the streets of Tiverton for the aero gang and other volunteers to canvass and see who had scrap items for the collection.

Instruction sheets were given as to how to wrap clothing, bind newspapers and magazines, and place metal for pickup. That gave everyone time to sort and be ready for December 28th, when the convoy of trucks, tractors, and cars would mobilize and deliver their gatherings to the railroad spur located behind the Balboa Oil tanks by the Sakonnet River.

Actually, scrap drives were old hat for Americans coming out of many years of the Depression. Yankee ingenuity and frugality seemed to come to the surface in hard times, and the citizens of the United States were experienced at taking tough times in stride. They knew how to sacrifice, save, and survive. They had grown victory gardens since the Great War and learned how to compost garbage or use it to feed livestock.

Meat shortages were commonplace, so when citizens got tired of fish, cheese, Spam, or just a plain ear of corn for a meal, a neighbor volunteer would go to Joe the Butcher, near the A&P in the Globe District of Fall River. Though he never would say where he got his meat, Joe must have had contacts with local farmers near Taunton and other local communities. He always seemed to be able to get the cut desired by his customers or would try hard to honor any request if he had a few days advance notice.

In the summer the Aero Gang was able to get a supply of sweet corn seeds so each could plant a garden either for food for their family or to sell for money at their temporary stand at the end of Haskins Avenue, next to Joe's stand. Often Joe and the neighbors were the primary customers, but in that summer of 1941, the gang's business had some competition across Highway 138, where some older kids from out of town decided to capitalize on the booming business and set up their own stand. Before long, the boys found themselves in a price war, and signs were erected to attract customers. At first, there was just a few pennies difference between the two businesses, but then Walter Peel introduced a beggars dozen, i.e., 13 to the dozen. The competition switched to 14 and lowered the price another 3 cents. Danny Lopez started to get angry and began telling the other group to relocate. The other group responded by throwing the culled wormy ears at the Aero boys, and they, in turn, responded in kind. Within minutes, the boys were involved in what would have been a snowball fight had it been winter. But it was early August, and this battle was personal for each member's family survival. Both sides were running across the road to get better shots and traffic had to slow down. Some cars stopped to watch the battle and were even cheering the kids on. There were ears of corn scattered everywhere, and Tommy and Toby were furiously trying to pick up the corn and put the ears in a bargain basket. This salvage effort only angered the others, and someone started throwing rocks. Bill ran to try to get Tommy out of the line of fire and was hit on the top of his head. Bill fell unconscious in front of Tommy, and instantly his blood trickled to the pavement. Tommy cradled his brother's head in his lap, and Joe got to their sides quickly as the other group jumped in a car and left quicker than they had arrived.

Mrs. Hobarth came to Bill's side and pressed her finger into the wound to stop the bleeding from Bill's head. As Bill regained consciousness, Joe said, "Billy we have to get you off the highway. Can you walk with me?"

Bill weakly replied, "I think so."

It was quite a sight as Bill walked home with the man with the crutch steadying him on one side and Mrs. Hobarth holding him on the other with her finger still on top of his head.

The rest of the gang cleaned up the area and continued with a banner sales day, thanks to the abundant resupply of corn provided by the competitors who were now out of business. The money was divided up, and as usual, a portion was set aside for Ernie to help with his expenses for the gang.

Back at home, Bill's mother fainted at the sight of all the blood, and Joe and Mrs. Hobarth had to continue to help by cutting Bill's hair around the wound, close the alcohol soaked wound with adhesive tape, and give him an ice pack to help with the swelling. Bill healed quickly and was a hero to all the gang who joked that, once again, he had used his head to help the gang!

Another alternative to the lack of meat was rattlesnake. Rhode Island was known for having a lot of rocky areas and a large population of snakes that came out to sun on the granite surfaces. The Balboa Oil company was planning to expand its tank farm along the shore and offered a bounty for rattlesnake heads and rattles to anyone who was willing to capture and kill rattlers before the construction crews had to deal with them. Not many people were willing to deal with the snakes but for Toby and his brother, Denny, and Tommy and Danny Lopez, it was exciting. It was also a good way to pick up some spare money, as well as a way to take home some alternative meat. When marinated and fried, or cooked on a grill, the snake could be served with a taste like a lot of other meats.

The hunting procedure was relatively simple. The boys would take a forked wild cherry branch of about 6 to 8 ft in length and, while Tommy or Danny were pinning the sunning snake behind the neck with the forked end of the stick, Denny or Toby would use a machete or ax to chop off the head of the snake. The boys knew to leave the heads alone for a while as they were known to bite right away, even without a body. Denny would cut off the rattles and place them in a knapsack, and the snake body would go into another larger, paper lined knapsack bag. Once all the snakes they could carry were harvested, Toby would go around with some old fireplace tongs and pick up the heads. He would place them in an empty metal oil container with a lid. The heads and rattles were taken to the Balboa Oil field office, and the boys usually showed off the snake bodies to the affable Mr. Sturtavant who always seemed to be as excited as the boys as he pulled out the 50 cents for each head and 10 cents for each rattle ring. He also offered $3.00 for a whole snake if the boys were not going to use them for food. The boys always took snaking, as they called it, very seriously and never once had a close call with the snakes.

Other survival skills included haircuts, done by Mom or Dad, and the ubiquitous "hand me down" clothing, forwarded from an older to a younger sibling or purchased from some church bazaar or a resale shop. Tires were retreaded, and cars and trucks were overhauled rather than sold. People automatically rationed their own gas and fuel oil. The way of life didn't really change much with the war. It just seemed more organized and purposeful. Scrap drives were more formal, but a fun way to feel like helping the war effort.

"I'm glad they waited till after Christmas. It gives everyone time to try to enjoy the holiday and clean things up afterward," said Kathryn Branner, as the boys sat down for some late night roast beef sandwiches and a piece of her special mince pie and milk after they returned from the full day of hiking around town. "Besides it gives the kids something to be excited about beyond Christmas. Lord knows it is a sad Christmas this year with families being pulled apart, as sons and daughters and husbands volunteer or get conscripted to the war. Not much peace on earth this year." she added.

"Yes, I heard that Steph next door joined the Navy and Harold Tarbert finally went to Canada and enlisted in their Air Corps," added Mr. Branner.

"Well, I'll be!" Billy exclaimed. "Wait till I tell the gang!

REALITY

Yes, it was true. Christmas 1941 was not a joyous time. Pearl Harbor's dead and wounded were still being reported, and there appeared a growing number of neighborhood homes with Blue Stars and Black Ribbons noting the passing of someone's son or husband. There were also many tears for young men and older men like Harold Tarbert and Stephy Stephinski who joined the Navy, Army, Marines, and a few hitched up with the Coast Guard and Merchant Marines. On top of that, the news was not good. The United States was getting clobbered on almost every front.

Although Wake Island valiantly held the Japanese at bay from December 7th to the 23rd, the remaining 450 men were forced to surrender and endure terrible hardships including beheadings and cannibalism by the Japanese. The battle for the Philippines started on December 8, 1941, and was not going well for the Americans. The biggest battle of all was just beginning and would last most of the war. The Battle of the Atlantic was the only battle that involved armed and unarmed civilian volunteers as well as the military. Even so, little things like a scrap drive did wonders for everyone, especially the youngsters. The older folks could volunteer for the USO, Red Cross, Civil Defense, or work for a defense industry. Women especially rallied to replace the men who left their jobs to go to war. But the kids needed to feel like contributing in any way and took over working on the farms, buying war bonds by purchasing 1 and 5 cent stamps at school and pasting them in their savings books. But scrap drives were more hands-on labor for the war effort and made everyone, especially the kids, feel like they were in the battle.

December 28th came and as early as 6:00 a.m., trucks and people started arriving at their designated streets. Mr. Ford brought his John Deere 'A' farm tractor with a large wagon attached with side rails and a wench. It was his assignment to collect the heavy items on any of the streets that had old iron fencing, car or truck parts, old anchors, or heavy engine blocks. He would lower a ramp, attach his winch, and, using his tractor's power take-off unit, pull the items onto his trailer. He was helped by a chain drive Mack coal truck from Bowen Oil and Coal which transported the heavier, bulky items lifted up by Mr. Ford's John Deer front loader.

Many people like Mr. Mortenstein volunteered their pickups, horse pulled hay racks, and cars to pick up the papers, magazines, and corrugated boxes. Most of the people who donated had everything tied in neat bundles, making it easier to load things quickly. Some of the gang would jump from the pickups and throw the items onto the trucks and others stayed on board to stack. The Branners were loaned a 1938 red Ford flatbed truck owned by O'Neil Brothers Construction. It had wooden side panel extensions that made it easier to stack papers and magazines, and there was a large tarp to hold down the load when it was full or if it were to rain. Toby Glavin usually rode with the Branners and would stuff comics and magazines under his shirt and jacket so he could look at them in their fort.

It was Toby who noticed one headline in a December 26th newspaper. He handed it to Bill to read: "President signs National Day of Thanksgiving Bill."

"Well, I'll be. He did sign it." Toby exclaimed. "Another no school day!!!" Tom and Bill joined in the laugh!

Once the trucks were full, they would make a beeline to the railway spur near the Balboa oil tanks to unload. The railroad cars were all labeled as to what was to be placed on board. Again, there were volunteers on board to try to neatly stack the respective items and use every available space on the railroad car. All the volunteers usually put in a full day, and often they were still loading the railcars into the early evening. Generally, these drives were held on Saturdays, and the boys would head for the fort early Sunday mornings to wait for the train to come, hook up to the cars, and haul them to Fall River, Boston, Providence or wherever the materials were processed for reuse. It was fun to see how many rail cars were filled with each drive, but, regardless of the number, every member of the Aero Gang usually slept well for at least two nights. It was a good feeling to help, and everyone worked together without argument or conflict. To the boys, it seemed to be an omen that America was going to win the war.

FREE TIME

December came and went, and at long last, the winter finally arrived in January 1942. The snow was a welcome change as the kids pulled their Flexible Flyers, Fleet Wings, and Thompson sleds out to the many hills in the area. Once again, the Aero Gang gravitated to the area of the Fort. Glavin's field and the Ford farm were nicely sloped for long rides on their sleds. The gang especially enjoyed it when the snow was good on weekends, as it allowed plenty of time to watch for the trains that would pass through their slope every few hours. They would each take turns putting their ears to the track to give warning to those sledding when they heard a train coming. On days when there was school, this was not as easy because there were usually fewer people to go sledding and less time to sled. Indeed, it was difficult to get home from school, change into old clothes, grab a sled, go to friends' houses, and head for the sledding hill. There was hardly time to enjoy an hour of sledding before the street lights came on and it was time for supper and homework.

On one occasion, when there was no extra person to listen for the train, Tommy, Toby, Swifty, Danny, Walter, and Bill had made an ice and snow jump over the railroad tracks that crossed their sledding hill. They then climbed to the top of the hill and made their own train by lining up their sleds, lying face down and hooking their toes into the fronts of the sled behind them. Bill went first, then Walter, Swifty, Toby, and Danny with Tommy sitting up as the caboose of the train. The usual procedure was to start as high on the hill as possible and, at about 100 yards, they would uncouple and individually, like good pilots, bank to the side, gain speed, and line up for the jump ramp one after the other.

The wind was blowing from the north, and no one could hear the northbound 5:00 train over the shouts and the chatter of the runners over the hardened snow. Since there were no crossings near the farm fields, the train never blew its whistle.

The boys went into their formation, broke off, and, with precision, executed their flawless jumps. Not even Tommy heard the train until it was on him, and he was in mid-air as the train blew through the boys jump ramp with a big cloud of snow. Tommy came flying out of the cloud in a perfect dead stick landing.

The boys ran to him laughing and congratulating him on his gutsy act. Apparently, when Tommy did finally see the train, he couldn't stop and just cleared the track in time as the engine's cowcatcher took out the jump. Tommy didn't know whether to laugh or cry, but he knew he was lucky to be alive. Out of worry that his parents would hear of this, Bill nervously stated to the boys that no one should talk about this episode or their sledding days would be over. He also suggested that they all go to the fort, light a fire, and make some hot chocolate so he would again be able to stress the importance of secrecy.

ON PATROL

It was 14 January, and U 87 was in a calm mid-Atlantic tethered to a service sub or "Milkcow" as the Germans called it. The sub gave U87 more fuel and replaced her antennas and floodlights damaged by Ernie, Robert, and Danny. U87's crew thoroughly cleaned Toby's gunked up periscope lens and cleaned the burn marks on her conning tower sail. Additional provisions and electric, radio, and sonar parts were also provided. U 87 was deemed fit for patrol and, following mutual Zeig Heil salutes to the Führer, parted company with the service sub. She then headed north to join its first wolf pack patrol in the North Atlantic. On 31 December 1941, she had little difficulty sinking the 8,200-ton British freighter, Cardita, but on January 17, 1942, she met stiffer opposition from the 8,000-ton Norwegian tanker, Nyholt, which was heavily armed. The Nyholt engaged U87 in a gun battle, badly damaging the sub before she went down from the sub's three torpedoes and deck gun damage. It took until January 30th for U87 to limp home to La Pallice, France for repairs.

Once U87's repairs were done, she began her second patrol on February 22, 1942. She was again assigned to the North American coast but was held in the western approach to support the Battleship Tripitz on convoy PQ12. After an uneventful patrol, U87 returned to St. Nazaire, France on March 27, to be refitted and await orders for another patrol.

APRIL LUCK

The war had not been going well for the United States. Despite the fact that the United Nations had signed a 26 nation declaration of support for the allied cause on January 1, 1942, Manila fell to the Japanese on the 2nd, and Dutch East India was attacked by the Japanese on January 11th. Leningrad evacuated its citizens on the 22nd of January to avoid the onslaught of the German Panzers. On the 25th of January, Thailand declared war on the United States and Bataan Fell to the Japanese on April 9th.

The late winter was slow to spring, but on April 18th came the good news of Doolittle's Raid on Tokyo, Japan. Though not as big as Pearl Harbor, damage wise, it was a moral victory for the folks at home. There had not been much good news, but it was the start of better news as the U. S. war effort kicked into gear. In just five months after Japan's surprise attack on us, we were now hitting back, and that really picked up American spirits. It seemed like you could actually feel the difference in people's affect. The boys in the Aero Gang started to meet again and talked about Doolittle's strategy and aircraft.

It was April 19, Tommy's birthday, and the gang was meeting at Ernie's for a special announcement. Tommy was with Bill, and the gang wished him a happy birthday, but since it was a serious time and Ernie had called the meeting, there was no cake or celebration. That would come later back at home.

As soon as everyone in the group, including D.B., arrived and settled into the usual tables and chairs and because everyone was asking about Robert, Ernie opened with a report about Robert's condition which was not good. As best as he could explain it, Robert had a bad infection all through his body and the doctors were trying new things to see if they could stop the continued lesions from forming in and on his body. Nothing seemed to be working so far, and he was now unable to have things like blankets on his body because of the pain from the blisters. No one could visit, but Ernie was going to try to arrange a phone call in the near future and allow each gang member the opportunity to talk to him, if possible. D.B. passed around a card and a fountain pen for everyone to sign their name, wishing him Godspeed. Then Ernie did something he had never done before. He called on those present to bow their heads in prayer and each, in their own way, offer a silent prayer for Robert. Ernie ended the silence with an "amen" and then, with a tear in his eye, he coughed, regained his composure, and told the boys about an idea he had and wanted their opinion.

Ernie continued, "I have a friend named Everet King who rides motorcycles with me and John Hodgson occasionally. He is from Falmouth, Massachusetts and has heard that this August there will be a Coastal Patrol based in Falmouth. That is not too far from us by air, and I am going to try to offer our services to be an auxiliary for Coastal Patrol 18 in Falmouth. It will give us more of a purpose to our activities and a place to fly to and from. If we are approved, we may be able to assist on some missions."

"What sort of missions?" asked Walter.

"Well, the Coastal Patrol is made up of volunteers who are helping the Navy and Coast Guard by assisting with search and rescue, cargo and courier service, target towing, border patrol, and serving as sub spotters and chasers," answered Ernie.

"Sub chasing. We've done that. In fact, we have done a little of all those things except target towing. But we have watched the Navy do it over Snake Island in the Bay." said Swifty

Ernie called for a decision by saying, "So how about it? Is this something I should shoot for?"

Bill answered, "Yes, we have wanted something like this for a long time. Too bad Robert and Harold are not here to get into the action right away. We don't have anyone really ready to fly, do we?"

"Walter and Swifty are close, and you are not too far behind, Bill. We have till August to get ready." answered Ernie and added, "Still, we will need to recruit more people. So, think about any of your friends with interest and bring them here for a meeting."

D.B. asked, "What do you think we should call this auxiliary?"

Ernie stated, "That may be determined by Coastal Patrol 18, but we still could name ourselves. Any ideas?"

"I have one. How about Robert's Wing Command?" chimed TC.

"That would be a nice gesture, Danny! Robert would be proud," D.B. added.

The group agreed, and Robert's Wing was formed.

Ernie also announced that he had finished repairs on 2 Ducky and would be flying to Falmouth tomorrow to propose his plan to the volunteers of Coastal Patrol 18 if anyone wanted to ride along. A forest of hands went up. Ernie laughed and chose Walter.

The next morning found Walter meeting Ernie at the Dartmouth Airport to do a walk around and preflight of 2 Ducky. As Ernie watched, Walter remembered Ernie's favorite expression; YOU CAN'T CHECK IT AT 90 MILES AN HOUR AND 3000 FEET. SO DO IT NOW!" Walter looked at everything including draining some fuel to check for water, making sure all the flaps and ailerons freely moved, taking the fuel cap off and checking to see if the tank was full, then making sure that the cap was back on and tight. He also made sure the tires had air and pulled the oil stick out to make sure she had clean and full oil. He then walked around the aircraft again to look at the fabric on the wings, fuselage, and float; making sure she was air and seaworthy with no stitching that looked weak or that there were no recent holes developing. Satisfied that everything was ok to fly, Walter looked up at Ernie who nodded and smiled and said, "Okay, now let's climb aboard and make sure she's ready on the inside as well."

"Yes, Sir!" answered Walter with a returning smile.

Upon completion of the basic checklist, Ernie surprised Walter with a loud shout out through the open side window of the canopy, "CLEAR!"

There was a sudden automatic cranking of the engine, and it immediately came to life

"You added an electric starter!" exclaimed Walter with an excited laugh.

"I was just getting ready to jump out to turn the crank."

"We still can if we need to but, if this continues to work, it is so much easier."

"I'll say!!" Walter said beaming.

"Okay Walter, take me to Falmouth," ordered Ernie.

"Yes, Sir! It isn't far so we should get there in two shakes of a lamb's tail!" chuckled Walter, as he gave her enough throttle to taxi to the end of the runway, stopped, revved her up, checked the magnetos, checked for any other traffic, and taxied into position on runway 9. He held, looked at Ernie who nodded, and Walter gave 2Ducky full throttle, held her down as the tail lifted, held her some more until she reached her take-off speed of 62 mph, and then gradually pulled back on the yoke and, up she went.

"Take a straight out departure and maintain a heading of 90 degrees and climb to 3500 feet out over the ocean. I want to radio the Falmouth airport, so they know we are on our way," said Ernie.

Ernie had earphones on and turned to Walter to say that Falmouth acknowledged and they were to "pattern for runway 08."

"Roger," Walter replied.

Within short order, Walter was entering crosswind and turning downwind, looking for traffic, and after extending downwind about three miles past the numbers so a plane could take off, he turned on base leg and then final with a perfect landing. He exited onto the taxiway and toward the airport building. Walter then turned the plane to face the field and cut the engine. "Very well done Walter! I think you are ready for some float training in the next few weeks. Let's see if these guys will buy our idea."

As they exited 2Ducky, they turned in time to see an old, black 36 Plymouth sedan pull up to them. A man rolled down the side window and asked if either of them was Ernie Gibson.

"I am he," said Ernie. "This is one of my wing pilots, Walter Peel."

Walter extended his hand, and the man did the same and, as they shook hands, the man said, "Nice landing, young man! I'm Captain Tibbs, the lead person for Patrol 18. Hop in, and we will drive to our hanger."

The hanger had an office and ready room. The hanger itself housed mostly Franklin powered Stinsons, all painted yellow and red. On the tarmac, there were three Fairchild 24's also painted yellow and red.

Captain Tibbs motioned for them to have a seat, as he said how much he liked the job done on 2Ducky. "We need more amphibious planes in our fold."

"Well, I have a wing that will have two available out of Tiverton with three other planes at Dartmouth. We can monitor your plane to ground communications and have phone services at both locations. When needed, I think our volunteers can respond and be in the air within 15 minutes to a half hour, depending on when called. We can't be a base like you, but we sure are ready to be an auxiliary for you." Ernie expounded.

"Sounds like it might work. What kind of experience do your volunteers have?" asked Gibbs.

"Living on and flying over the ocean, we are very experienced at spotting, so I am certain we could help with shore observation, search and rescue, sub monitoring, and courier/cargo services," Ernie continued.

"Sounds like you have been organized for a while."

"Yes, for about seven years and I have trained all our pilots myself."

"What made you start that far back?"

"Billy Mitchell convinced me that we would need pilots, sir."

"Right you are, and more people should have listened to him. It is a shame he was court marshaled for sinking that target ship with a plane. Now we are trying to catch up. Where did you get your training?"

"I flew Spads with Rickenbacker in the First War, sir."

"Well, I'm sold, and I think we can put something together. We are in the process of changing our structure from three regions to a base system like the military. It looks like it is more centralized, but it really gives each base more autonomy to do what you are proposing. We hope to be activated in the latter part of August, and we will definitely let you know. Getting five more aircraft, with two of them amphibious, is a real find, not to mention having extra personnel to boot. We will definitely be in touch. Let me give you a lift back to your plane and, if it's not too much to ask, perhaps you could let me have a look?"

"Most certainly!" answered Ernie.

As they rode back to the plane, Ernie asked if Tibbs was connected to the Katherine Tibbs School of Business.

"Why yes. How did you know?" Tibbs asked.

"I have been attending classes periodically to try to improve my cabinet and furniture business in Tiverton. I thought you looked familiar. Tell Katherine her classes have helped. Thanks again for your time, Captain. Robert's Wing looks forward to hearing from you in August."

"No doubt about it. We will be in touch for certain, and it is Gordon, Ernie," Tibbs said as he extended his hand with a sincere smile.

Ernie and Walter both shook hands with Tibbs and climbed into the plane. Once inside, Walter turned to Ernie and said, "Ernie, I knew you flew in the war, but I didn't know you flew with Rickenbacker."

"Yea, we had to have been in the air at the same time, and I'm sure I waved to him once or twice," Ernie replied dryly. "What about it?

Walter just laughed and said, "You really sold him! You must know something I don't. How are we going to find another amphib and two more planes and three more pilots?" Walter asked nervously.

Ernie just smiled confidently and said, "Swifty knows where every available plane is in three states, and we have you, Swifty, and Bill Branner on deck for pilots, so I'm not worried. Besides, I have more pilot friends who have expressed interest in volunteering. Now," Gibson ordered, "Let's go home."

R.C.A.F.

At the family dinner gathering in London, Ontario, Harold Tarbert sat between his mother and Lisa Clarkson, an attractive teenager who, like many, was a Home Front volunteer and very interested in everything Harold had to say. Indeed, Canada was not unlike the U.S., in that there was a near-reverent empathy for the military men and women, and they were treated well by everyone. For the first time in his life, he was relaxed and easily engaged in conversation with a young lady. As the meal came to a close, Lisa left to help with desserts, and Harold immediately entered into lengthy conversation with Robby Clarkson, Lisa's brother. Robby's sandy brown hair was closely cut in a military style haircut which seemed to accentuate his greenish eyes and frequent white tooth smile. He was a muscular, medium height private of 19, who was stationed out of Halifax with a Canadian RAF squadron of Lockheed Hudson bombers. Before the war, they did a variety of tasks for supplying some of the native people in the northern provinces and the Royal Canadian Mounted Police, but now they were primarily assigned to coastal patrol to protect ships from submarines as they formed up for convoys to Britain. Robby said that they had perfected various techniques for dropping depth charges from the air, and he was getting the first-hand experience as a bombardier in addition to being a gunner. He added that a pilot friend of his named Nick Small from his RCAF Squadron 113 had sunk U754 on July 31, 1942, north of Boston. Filling him with all kinds of exciting experiences about the Lockheed Hudsons, Robby had Harold sold before the family meal was over. Robby said he knew that they were looking for pilots with experience and thought that Harold could quickly work his way through multi-engine and combat training in three or four months. He also said

122

that he could introduce Harold to the right people and get him signed up if Harold would return with him to Halifax.

"Harold, I can't tell you what to do. I know it is a tough decision. I didn't know what to do either, but when Jamie, my older brother, enlisted in the Navy, I started thinking more seriously about serving. Kind of funny, eh? Jamie is serving on the St. Croix, one of our destroyers assigned to protect our convoys in the Atlantic. He's dropping depth charges from the sea, and I'm dropping them from the air. One of us should get lucky, sometime." Robby added, "The food is good, the barracks are clean, you get uniforms, and you get paid. It is not much but you really have no expenses to speak of, and you can send the money you earn home to your Mom like I do for Kent and Carol, my Dad and Mom. All you have to do is fly, or in my case, drop bombs and shoot." he added with a laugh.

Lisa returned to the table and amended what Robby had to say by adding that they had other family members in the Royal Canadian Navy serving, like Jamie on Convoy Patrol. "One such relative, named Ross "Knobby" Clarkson had been assigned to the CRN Matane to escort convoys to Murmansk, Russia for close to five years. His wife, Pearl, wrote to him nearly every day and spent time crocheting a pillow with his name and Matane on it. Everyone was doing what they could to keep our fighting men's spirits up in their quest to stop Hitler. Having Harold in RCAF was bound to help!" she added with a brief hug of enthusiasm. Harold turned bright red but enjoyed the moment.

That evening when Robby stepped outside of his family's home at 199 Victoria Street to board the bus to the train station, Lisa joined Harold as he carried his own suitcase toward the bus stop. Climbing on the bus, Harold turned to Lisa and bid her goodbye with a rather stiff handshake and addressed his astonished mother, who had followed him to the door of the bus, saying, "Don't worry, Mom. I know I am a senior and all, but I can finish high school when the war is over. This is what I need to do, and I know it. I will write daily to keep you posted on what I am doing.

You can share the letters with Ernie and the gang. Take care. Love you!" With that, he turned, stepped into the bus as the door closed behind him, and the bus pulled out into the barren, fog-enshrouded street.

Everything Robby said proved to be true. Ernie was right too. Harold was a quick learner and an excellent student pilot. By February he had earned his wings and was logging flight hours in the right seat in Lockheed Hudsons. By the end of April, he was finally a pilot in command of his own plane, "Robert's Wing" and was assigned to convoy patrol between Halifax and Iceland.

FOUND

It didn't take Swifty long to locate another Duck. He and Ernie had agreed that is what should be looked for because of everyone, including the mechanics at Dartmouth, was now familiar with that type of aircraft.

"I found one, Ernie!" Swifty said with excitement in his voice. "It's in Hartford, and they say it flies. They want $1200 for it, and that will be a bargain if we don't have to do too much to it once we get her home."

"Well, I guess we had better make plans to go see it, so we know. I'll give them a call," Ernie said, grabbing the listing out of Swifty's hands for the phone number.

While Ernie contacted the phone operator to connect him to the number in Hartford, Swifty dashed back to the Aero Gang's meeting area at the back of Ernie's shop to fill the guys in on the news. They all waited quietly in suspense until Ernie came back to them after about a half hour. They could tell it was a go by the smile on Ernie's face as he said, "Walter, I want you and Bill to do something to widen 2 Ducky's seats so we can carry four people to Hartford. If our new bird will fly, we will bring her back and you two will fly 2Ducky back while Swifty and I will nurse the other bird home. Also, I will set out a few basic tools in a tool box that will fit in that storage bay we made in the flotation hull. Bill make sure that it gets in there, so we have tools if we need them."

"I will," answered Bill. "When are we scheduled to go?"

"This Sunday at 0800. We will meet up at Dartmouth." Ernie answered.

Walter asked all the guys to give him ideas for material for the seats.

TC responded first by saying, "My Dad has a wooden, double wide, fold up chase lounge that might work. Just take off the lower sections, so you don't interfere with the rudders. You could use exhaust brackets to clamp it tight through the holes in the existing seat, and you can tie in some cushions to keep your backsides from getting numb. Trouble is I only have one, and you can't mess it up because my Dad likes his lounge chair. Try to return it in one piece, or you will be buying him a new one."

"No problem," answered Walter. "Can you bring the whole chair out to the airport tomorrow so we can work on it? Let's get an early start in case we have problems. Say 6:00? I have a hunch that we can use the lower portion to design a chair for the back seat as well. We have clamps at the shop in Dartmouth, and the guys there will lend a hand if need be."

"I don't know if I can get a ride cuz my Dad doesn't get much gas with the rationing system," TC said.

Bill inserted that he thought either his mom or dad or D.B. would help. Then he added, "I don't know about Sunday. We have something planned at church, I think,"

Ernie answered with a wink. "I will call your mom and tell her that you are invited to come with me to see my church. Heck, if that doesn't work we will climb to 5000 feet, and you can talk to God yourself! But you are going to be with us, for sure, Bill."

Bill and the gang laughed and the excitement of the trip improved everyone's mood.

The next morning saw a red Studebaker honking at TC's house. DB had joined the Red Cross and was active as a volunteer in the U.S.O., so she had more gas rations available than the Branners, who used most of their allotment going to and from work and for their weekend trips to Boston to see Robert. The lounge just barely fit in the trunk, but they got it in, and Bill tied down the lid. TC, Bill, and DB headed for the airport. On the way, they stopped at the Hummingbird for a quick donut breakfast with Caty.

Then they stopped at Ernie's shop to get the toolbox. They pulled into the airstrip at five to seven, and Walter was already in 2Ducky sizing things up. Bill and Danny brought him the lounge, and they started pulling the lounge apart and inserting the better section into the front seat. Bill made sure the tools were in the storage compartment as he had promised Ernie and then walked over to the mechanics' shed to tell the guys about the new Duck they were going to look at in Hartford. The mechanics were glad to hear the news and made plans to be back at the airfield late Sunday afternoon so they could have a look if the boys were to bring her into the hanger. After about an hour, the seats had been modified, but they were not sure about the lap belts. Instead of forcing both front and back occupants to suck it in and share one lap belt, they talked to the mechanics about how to add anchors so two more belts could be added. The mechanics had some used belts from damaged planes and took over with the installation. Walter said he would tell Ernie that it was good to have the extra belts in the event that they had to set down in the ocean and pick up survivors. He might even want to keep the seats if they were comfortable.

"Then you will buy my Dad another chair?" Danny asked.

"Yes, we promised you that yesterday," stressed Walter. TC looked relieved.

"Are you men ready to head back now?" asked DB, who had come back from a few hours of work with the Red Cross.

"Ok then, hop in Baker, and we'll be off. I'll bet you are excited about going to Hartford tomorrow."

"You bet," they answered in unison.

"Wish I was going too," said TC.

"Hey TC, there's room on the float. We could tie you on!!" Walter said with a hearty laugh!

"Funny man!" TC replied.

Recognizing the hurt look on Danny's face, Bill added, "Don't worry Danny. You know Ernie is fair. You will get your chance soon, I'm sure."

BLUE YONDER

Even though he wasn't going along, TC was 'Johnny on the spot' first thing Sunday morning and had 2Ducky out of the hanger and fueled and ready for the trip to Hartford as the rest of the gang started showing up. It was always interesting on weekends because the boys' families tended to take more of an interest by driving them out and staying for the takeoff.

Branners were in Boston, but D.B. brought Bill, and Tommy and Toby were in the back seat of Baker. Mr. Peel brought Walter and Mr., and Mrs. Swift brought Swifty. Even Danny's dad hitched a ride to see how his lounge was being pressed into special service. He told Ernie not to worry about returning it if it worked. He was glad to contribute something to the Coastal Patrol. Ernie smiled and said thank you, knowing that Mr. L, as the boys called him, did not have much to give.

"We appreciate everything that comes our way Mr. L. Thank you!" Ernie said as he shook Mr. Lopez's hand in gratitude.

"By the way, Ernie, how are you paying for the other plane if you decide to buy it?" asked Mr. Swift.

"Oh, like most everything so far, it comes out of my business. This time I took out a loan, so I am certain to have the cash if I go with a big purchase. My business is my collateral."

"That's taking a rather big risk isn't it?" asked Mr. Swift.

"Not with these boys it isn't. They never let me down." Ernie reflected with pride.

"Well you sure have made a big impression for the good with Swifty, and we want to thank you for all you have done." As he shook Ernie's hand, Ernie felt a piece of paper being pressed into the palm of his hand. Thinking it was a thank you note, he just put it in his pocket. It wasn't till much later that he realized that it was a 100 dollar bill with a piece of notepaper attached with the words "Down Payment" written on it.

Ernie turned to the boys and said, "Walter you have some air time already with 2Ducky, and you will be flying her back if we buy the plane. I want Swifty in the front with me going, so he gets some time to feel how she performs. You and Bill take the back seat, and let Bill follow the controls on this trip and on the return."

"Roger!" answered Walter.

Ernie continued, "Bill, walk us through the preflight. Danny just might have missed something. Remember," and just as he was about to say it, all the boys said laughingly, "You can't check it at 90 miles an hour at 3000 feet so DO IT NOW!!" Bill led the walk around and covered everything except the tires, and Walter reminded him by checking them himself. Once that was done, Ernie raised the canopy, and they all climbed into their respective seats.

Ernie shouted out, "NICE JOB, DANNY!!" and waved to Danny who was standing back with the rest of the spectators. Before he could close the canopy, the plane wiggled, and there stood D.B. with two small baskets.

"Caty and I made some sandwiches for you in case you find time to eat." The boys' faces lit up because Caty was known for her great sandwiches at the Hummingbird. She added, "Good luck and have a safe trip guys!!!" and stepped off the plane and returned to stand beside Tommy and Toby who were waving. Ernie turned around to the back seat and said, "Bill, it is time for you to visit my church! Swifty, let's run through the checklist and fire her up."

Within a few more minutes, 2Ducky was roaring to life and taxiing to runway 27 for a straight out departure. Swifty was quick with the throttle and the roll, tail lift, and take off, smoothly transitioning them to flight. At 2000 feet, Ernie had Swifty bank her into a right 360-degree turn, and the boys saw Lincoln Park, the War College, Mt Hope Bridge, Newport Navy Yard, and the PT Boat training area. Off in the distance was the Cinanicut River near Jamestown, Fort Wetherill, and Fort Adams across from

Newport, the Newport Harbor, and the East Passage of Narraganset Bay. Across the bay, Ernie pointed out the eight groups of mines and a submarine barrier set up by the 1200 man 243rd Coastal defense regiment. Though their bunkers were camouflaged, at 2Ducky's altitude, it was relatively easy to see the alignment of 12 inch, 6 inch, and 3-inch gun batteries together with anti-aircraft batteries and 50 caliber machine gun batteries aligning the 11000-yard east passage that was open for shipping. Further west were four similar groups of mines and a western passage with another regiment's guns on the Warwick side of the bay near the Quonset Point Naval Air Station. "It would be quite a roar if they all decided to practice at once, but they alternate turns, so the citizens don't get alarmed." Ernie said, and added, "We have probably one of the best-protected bays on the east coast. If the Germans want to try to get in here, they will have to deal with Rhode Island grit!

Bill asked Ernie, "Do those guys down there know we are on their side?"

Ernie answered with a smile, "There are three reasons we are safe, Bill. One, I got clearance by calling them and telling them exactly when we would be flying over. Two, we are in a yellow and red plane. No camouflage for us. We want to be seen. Three, we are in one of the ugliest planes ever produced, and the Germans would not be caught dead in one."

The boys laughed as Swifty headed for Providence and further inland before heading southwest for Hartford Airport.

Ernie continued his tour with some helpful piloting instructions by saying, "You can keep those New York, New Haven, and Hartford railroad tracks off your left wing tip and you will be in line to enter the pattern when we get to Hartford."

After about an hour of flying, Swifty noticed that the airspeed indicator had slowed and asked Ernie about it. Ernie told him to look for flags, windsocks, or smoke to see if the wind had changed direction. The boys saw smoke from a stack and noticed that the wind had changed and was now coming as a stiffer land breeze out of the west.

"That is okay because we will soon be slowing as we approach Hartford, but we will be left of pattern and extending, so we can make a gradual 180 and enter downwind, cross, and turn on final for 27. There is no civilian traffic with the war, but there are a few commercial flights and lots of military but not so much at this airport.

We are close to ten miles out, so I am going to report that I am entering their airspace with the intention on landing. I will ask if there is traffic. If there is no answer, there is either no traffic or no one near the radio. Help me look for traffic."

There was no answer.

"Swifty, I am taking control of the aircraft."

The landing was smooth and uneventful. The boys spotted a Duck like theirs and Ernie taxied over to it and parked alongside. The boys jumped out and attached their tie-down cords to the anchor hooks in the tarmac.

Ernie announced that they were about ten minutes early, so he broke out the sandwich baskets and had a short debriefing discussion about the flight. It didn't take long for the sandwiches to disappear, and before long an airport jeep pulled up, and a man got out.

"I'm Mat Rock, the owner of the Duck. Want to have a look?"

With that, the boys all began to do what they knew best, a preflight inspection and walk around. Ernie opened the cowling and checked the engine for any tell tail leaks or excessive carbon markings.

"She is due for an engine overhaul, but with the war, I have neither the time nor the money to fly her, let alone maintain her. That is why I'm selling her. She is a good aircraft, and we have always had good service out of her. We hate to let her go, but after the war, we may be able to buy a new one. What are you planning on using her for?"

"We are members of Coastal Patrol Base 18 out of Falmouth, Massachusetts and specifically an auxiliary, amphibious base in Tiverton, Rhode Island, and we intend to use her to hunt for subs and do search and rescue work," answered Ernie.

Mr. Rock looked impressed and said, "Really? That is something. My plane after subs and saving airmen and seamen. Care to take her up before you decide?"

"I reckon. I would," answered Ernie.

He and Swifty took off leaving Walter and Bill to talk with Mr. Rock.

"My Dad is with Firestone, and they are producing all kinds of things for the war. What sort of work do you do Mr. Rock?" Bill asked.

"I am with the Colt Firearms Company. We are also pretty busy now with the war effort; primarily 45 cal pistols for the Army and Marines.

"You boys seem pretty young to be pilots. How long have you been flying?"

"Oh, we have been with Ernie for about five years, and he has taught us everything to this point. We are getting experience now, so if we have to go to war, we can enlist and fly when we are of age," answered Walter.

Just then Ernie did a touch and go and took her straight up to a full power stall, recovered, reentered the pattern, touched down and taxied over to 2 Ducky. Climbing out of the aircraft, Ernie was all business saying,

"You're right. She is a sound aircraft. Now, about the price and the possibility of payments. We are a low budget; all-volunteer operation and do not have a treasury to speak of. Can you give us any consideration? We will be painting her our yellow with red trim, and that, together with the overhaul, will set us back a bit."

Mr. Rock thought for a moment and then said,

"Tell you what, you complete the overhaul and painting and bring her back to show me what you have done to our plane, and I will donate her to your cause. Technically, she is owned by Colts, and I have been flying and maintaining her. I think we can get some positive publicity when we see her all painted and ready for a donation to such a good cause. How about that?"

The boys just stood there with their mouths open and not saying a word. Ernie, too, was speechless at first and then asked if they could put the agreement in writing, so there is no confusion. He then added, "Here is one hundred dollars as good faith money that we will be back with your brand spanking new plane."

Mr. Rock reached into his vest pocket and pulled out a notepad and pen. He began writing; "Received from Ernie Gibson one hundred dollars as earnest money toward the $1200 purchase price of the 1934 Colt Firearms Company's Duck aircraft. The Colt Company intends to donate the plane upon completion of an overhaul and painting by Mr. Gibson's Coastal Patrol Wing."

He signed the note Mathew Rock, President, Colt Firearms and handed it to Ernie saying, "Just tell me when it is ready so I can gather the big wigs and press, and the $100 will be here waiting for you. How about a last taxi ride to the terminal?"

Ernie and Swifty gave Mr. Rock his last ride in his plane and bid him goodbye while Walter and Bill fired up 2Ducky for the ride back to Tiverton. They purposely stayed over land all the way back, as it was growing late in the April sky.

The return flight was perfect in every way, and the mechanics at the airport were all over the plane once it was in the hanger. Ernie and the boys decided to go to the Hummingbird and celebrate by having dinner and calling their family and other gang members.

While they were eating, Ernie slipped into the back room and called the Boston Children's Hospital and asked for Robert Branner's room. Kathryn Branner answered and said that Robert's condition was better today, and she thought having phone conversations with the gang might perk him up a little more. Ernie dragged the black phone cord over to the boys' table and handed the phone to Bill Branner first. Immediately, everyone knew that Ernie was keeping his promise to call Robert, and the gang got real quiet as Bill talked.

"Robert? Doesn't sound like you. How are you? I know it is hard for you to talk, so I will pass the phone around for everyone to give you some news. We got another plane today like 2Ducky. Yeah, we flew to Hartford and picked it up. Walter and I flew 2 Ducky back. Walter will be getting his wings soon. Swifty too. Me? I have a way to go yet, but I'm trying. We are going to be a part of the Falmouth Coastal Patrol come August, so we are getting ready for that. Here's Tommy!"

Tommy took the phone which looked rather large in his hand and against his face, but right away he said,

"Hi, Robert! We had a scrap drive for the war, and we really worked hard for you. Hope you are feeling better and can come home soon." Tommy passed the phone over to TC, who just started crying at how sorry he was. If he hadn't made the bomb, they might not have had the accident. Robert put him at ease with his calm voice saying,

"If we hadn't had the bomb, we might have been blown from the sky sooner. You shouldn't worry and blame yourself."

Danny just sobbed and handed the phone to Swifty who told him about getting the new plane and handed it off to Walter who told Robert how smooth Ernie was at negotiating with the Coastal Patrol and Colts for the new plane. Robert really laughed at the part about Ernie flying with Eddie Rickenbaker. Everyone got up and left the table when the phone was handed to D.B. who, in spite of her years, had a hard time talking without tears as Robert explained to her that he was not too sure he was going to pull out of this. He had a lot of pain, but the memories of her really helped and that he wanted to see her again if she could make the trip with his folks sometime. She explained that she was in the USO and Red Cross but would plan a time to come to Boston the first chance she got. She remembered that Toby hadn't talked, so she called him over, and he sat in her lap and let him listen while Robert said,

"Hello, Toby."

Then Toby said, "Ya know what Robert? We are naming our Coastal Patrol Robert's Wing, so in a way, you are still with us. We think of you all the time and really miss you. Get better will ya?" With that, he left D.B., and they continued to talk for a few minutes. Then DB said goodbye and hung up the phone. Everyone seemed to have watery eyes as they all headed for home.

TOWING

Walter and Swifty got their wings within days of each other, and Ernie taught them how to tow targets for the Navy to practice their shooting. Ernie personally went to the commanding officers to talk to them about the boys and how special they were. No hot shot was to play it too close to his boys, or they could just shoot at seagulls for all he cared. "Our planes are red and yellow, and the tow targets are painted to look like German planes. 500 to 1,000 ft tow line should be enough for safe practice. There should be no confusion." The CO assured him that extra care would be taken to assure their safety.

Early the next morning Walter hooked up his tow and headed out over the anti-aircraft zone of the 243rd near the eastern passage of the bay. He was instructed to vary his altitude starting at 5,000 ft. and dropping down 500 ft. with each pass. Noticing that they were not even coming close to hitting the target, he kept staying in the pattern longer. At 1,500 ft., there still were no hits, so Walter dropped to about 100 ft. and just about put the tow target in their laps. The artillery battalion was so surprised that they opened up with anti-aircraft and 50 mm machine gun fire, disintegrating the target. After that day the men with the guns and Walter seemed to have an understanding. If Walter was going to expend time and gas flying targets, he expected them to "hit the dang thing."

Swifty had a lot of respect for the fighter pilots out of Quonset Point and was excited to be towing for them. From his vantage point, he envied the dive bombers and torpedo bombers as they practiced dropping on the ship like image of Snake Island, not far from Stone Bridge. His problem was a little different in that he was never sure of where the interceptor pilots were going to pounce on his tow. He was instructed to pretend to be an invader from the ocean at different altitudes, and they would come out of the sun or up from the ocean or straight on. Either way, the men from Quonset would scare the bejebes out of him and usually hit the tow. He especially appreciated it when, after the practice, some of the pilots would come along beside him and give him a thumbs up or a salute of thanks.

So, for far different reasons, the two tow men would spend the next few months towing after school and on weekends and then meet in the ready room for a Coke or coffee to try to calm down after a "mission." Still, from Ernie's perspective, it was good experience and would help them in their future when or if they were needed in the military.

William, or Bill, was another story. He flew ok, but it was less natural and more methodical. Bill always liked plotting and flight planning and looking for things in the air. Ernie decided to bring him along for "search and rescue" practice, and before long he was riding with Ernie on practice and actual missions. Bill had excellent long-range vision and could spot a bird flying at altitude in enough time to avoid hitting it. Bill always knew where he was, and hence he was a natural navigator. If a call came in to go look for someone, Bill would have it plotted by the time TC or someone had the plane ready, and it would be Bill and Ernie who would head out.

At the end of May, the gang got another member named Donald Schnell. Donald had started school with the gang but moved away and had now returned and was finishing high school at Durfee High in Fall River. He had heard about the Coastal Patrol and had stopped at the Dartmouth airport to inquire. He had learned to fly in the Boston area and was already a licensed pilot, so Ernie signed him up and put him on the tow detail and pulled Swifty and Bill for the search and rescue practice.

Donald seemed to fit into the Robert mold in that he was rather shy, yet handsome, freckled faced, curly-haired, blond and, according to Ernie, a very good pilot. The gang seemed to enjoy his return, and he just slipped into the role of being the lead pilot.

It didn't take long for Donald to have success. It was 3 July 42, and the other members of the gang were doing other assignments when Donald heard the call from Falmouth for sub spotting assistance east of Boston. He got Ernie's approval over the phone and was airborne within 10 minutes and, in short order, was at 5,000 ft. altitude making S turns as he proceeded east to west over the bay. Donald had no formal military training, but he had watched the Navy flyers training with bomb runs on Snake and Spar Island in Mt. Hope Bay. He was also an avid student of books about artillery and bombing strategies and that, coupled with lengthy discussions with Ernie and some of the pilots at Quonset Naval Air Station, bolstered his confidence that he knew what to do. He even had practiced with Ernie using lime bag bombs on Snake Island like the Navy did.

Suddenly he saw the sub boldly running on the surface. He broadcasted his position for the Navy and Coast Guard and dove on the sub, determined to plant his aluminum marker "bombs" right on its tower. As he had practiced with Ernie, he dove so he would pull out at about 500 ft. of altitude and a quarter mile behind the sub. The U boat had seen him and was starting its dive just as his three markers hit its deck and sail. He was proud of himself but wished he had a few 100 pounders to cause some damage to keep the sub on the surface. Even so, a British antisubmarine trawler, HMS Le Tiger, responded to Donald's identity call and was close to the markers. With the trawler's sonar and the help of the little red and yellow plane, it was able to quickly search and destroy U 215. Donald headed back to a hearty hero's welcome by the gang at Dartmouth.

Ernie was feeling like Robert's Wing was starting to jell into a solid unit. Following Donald's example, the Aero Gang willingly took on any assignment Ernie gave them and did well. Everyone was able to do each other's duties, and each one had a specialty as well. Colonial Tibbs was able to steer Ernie toward a few pilots with planes, and Ernie set it up for the owners to agree to allow others to fly them as well.

It was the end of July, and Robert's Wing was now fully trained, fully staffed, and ready to be pressed into service. It was time to communicate with Colonial Tibbs again, and Ernie decided to do a fly in to meet the men of the 18th.

THE THIRD PATROL

U87's refitting and repair was completed in early May, and by the 19th she was back on patrol again in the New England waters. As she approached Boston, she placed a series of 15 mines and laid in wait for ships forming up for convoys to Britain. The opportunity finally came the second week in June, when Captain Bruger and his crew noticed an increase in shipping activity as Convoy XB25 started to gather off of the Canadian coast. The Canadians had very heavy protection with Navy destroyers and patrol boats and a constant umbrella of air surveillance. Bruger considered the options and decided to wait until the convoy got underway. On June 16th Bruger identified two ships, the 8400-ton freighter, SSPort Nicholson, carrying 2 million troy ounces of platinum, and the 5900 ton Cherokee, carrying industrial freight. Berger fired two torpedoes, and the Cherokee went under in six minutes with the Port Nicholson taking closer to six hours before she went down. U87 submerged in the darkness and evaded convoy defenses for several days. Then, in the early dawn hours of June 22nd, just off Cape Cod, a small amphibious red and yellow plane spotted the sub on the surface near Provincetown. The pilot with a heavy southern drawl dialed to 121.5 on his radio and made an open to all, early morning, fog-enshrouded broadcast; "Enemy submarine heading north of Cape Cod on the surface. I will continue to maintain a ten-mile radius to assist military location. This is 2Ducky standing by."

Almost immediately there was a reply from a Canadian bomber group of Lockheed Hudson bombers returning from flying protective convoy cover.

"2 Ducky, is that you Swifty? Over."

"Roger that. Harold? Over."

140

"I'm coming up behind and above you at two o'clock and have you in sight. Where's the sub? Over."

"Last sighted through fog about 10 miles northwest of my position at approximately 10 o'clock. Over."

"You sure he's not friendly? Over."

"He's got a talon on his tower, Harold. He is either crippled, or he didn't see me when I first saw him. Tried to get him to think I was moving away. Over."

"Good thinking. Talon eh? That's Robert's Sub! Let's get him."

"Roger, you've got the bombs. I just have the eyes and not much fuel. I need to break off and head back. Good Luck, Harold!"

"Roger. Will do! See you again, Swifty! Thanks!!"

"Robby, You on track?" Harold asked.

"Roger."

"She's all yours, then!"

Within seconds of breaking through the morning fog, Robby saw the sub starting a dive and corrected his course to intercept the sub's track. Robert's Wing bobbed up as Robby let loose its load of bombs and depth charges and the other bombers in the formation followed suit. They saw the sub turn sharply to starboard as she dove deep, as the ocean erupted in a continuous blossoming of foam from the depth charges. The bombers circled the area and noted an oil slick and some debris but saw no definite verification of a kill. With no extra depth charges or bombs available and low fuel, Harold and the rest of the 113 squadron could not linger and were forced to return to base at Halifax. U87 had been lucky once again.

WOUNDED

"I knew that red and yellow plane had seen us! Emergency dive! All ahead full!" Captain Bruger took her as deep as he could, but the depth charges damaged the rear torpedo doors, and U87 was taking on water in her rear compartment. He ordered his men to move forward and seal off the rear torpedo room.

"Steering is sluggish, sir." said the helmsman.

Bruger had no choice but to jettison more oil and debris and hope that the Canadians or the Americans would leave his sub alone. Once again the fog, depths, and evasive maneuvers were his friends, and he flooded his forward ballast to keep his ship level at 80 meters and limped his way toward the deeper Atlantic waters.

"Sir we cannot run this deep. We are taking on water throughout the sub," said the helmsman.

Bring her up to 50 meters and see if the leaking slows!" Bruger ordered.

Aye Captain."

After several suspense-filled minutes, the helmsman reported again, "Sir, all stations report the leaks are slowing."

"Good, I think we are going to try Wilhelm's snorkel. If it doesn't work, we can surface tonight, check the damage, and try to keep out of everyone's sight and run on the surface, if we can.

"We need to find a place to try to make repairs. I will call for a Milkcow sub if there is one to be had, but I doubt it."

"Christian, if you and your 'friends' had not made such a scene back in Rhode Island, we could sneak back there for repairs, but they probably have sealed off that option by now."

Christian thought for a moment and said, "What about Rhode Island Sound where the only traffic is that stupid ferry boat. We know her schedule and can be on the surface at night for repairs and submerge when it is time for the ferry!"

142

"That might work, Christian!" replied Bruger, as a look of hope seemed to reduce the stress lines on his face. You just may get your own boat if we can pull this off and not have to go back to France for refitting again!"

The idea worked to a limited extent in that their primitive snorkel worked, and Berger's excellent crew was able to make repairs to the rear torpedo doors, but the other leaks proved to be too detailed for surface repair by the crew. U87 was forced to return to France on July 8th.

CAP

The August deadline finally arrived, and Ernie contacted Colonial Tibbs and invited him and other members of Coastal Patrol 18 to an August 30th meeting at Dartmouth Airport. 2Ducky was docked in Tiverton so the guests could get a feel for the auxiliary services they would have available to them. The Coastal Patrol was now to be called the Civil Air Patrol, and all members of Robert's Wing were sporting black baseball style caps with gold embroidered badge stitching announcing membership of:

The Tiverton CAP, mostly known as Robert's Wing, did its best to present its capabilities. At the Dartmouth Airport, TC had the red and yellow 1Ducky ready on the tarmac with 5 other private planes lined up in formation behind 1Ducky. There was a formal tour of the facilities at Dartmouth, and a visit to 2Ducky at the water base behind Ernie's cabinet shop in Tiverton. It was an impressive setting and, for those in attendance, there was unanimous agreement that Falmouth and Tiverton should work together. That opportunity would soon come.

A DAY FOR COLTS

August 31st was the day 1Ducky was to be in Hartford to meet with the Colt Firearms top brass and the press. Ernie felt it was time to give TC some time, so he chose Danny to accompany him to Hartford and allowed him to take control of the aircraft part way through the trip. T.C. was on cloud nine most of the time, as Ernie explained how much he appreciated his assistance with the maintenance of the aircraft and helping the gang get ready for flights.

"I didn't help Robert much though, Ernie. Sure wish he could be here to share how far we have come."

"Yea, me too. But that event is what has pushed us to this point. Before that, we were just a bunch of guys in an Aero club. We learned a lot from that and got serious about the war. I just wish more of our soldiers and sailors knew how much of an effort you young guys and the Civil Air Patrol were contributing to keep America together, so they have something to come home to. You, Robert, D.B., and the guys are in this fight, and I feel good about what we are doing. History will tell the story of how much we did. You need to be proud of that, Danny!"

"I am, but I get a little down at times."

"We all do at times. But the tough just keep at it and the successes and good times make it all worthwhile. You'll see!"

Ernie landed 1Ducky at Hartford to the flashing cameras of the press and, after a speech by Mr. Rock returning the $100 check; a small band played Wild Blue Yonder.

Ernie then turned to Danny and said, "Do the preflight, get in the front seat and start the Duck. I will jump in when you wave and say it is ready."

One of the reporters asked, "You are letting HIM fly the Duck?" implying that Danny's mixed race might make him incapable.

145

Ernie spun toward the man and said, "Yes sir, he is one of the best in our wing. Just watch us take off and put that in your paper."

Danny motioned for Ernie to get in, which he did, and from the back seat told Danny to follow him through. Ernie reported to the tower and requested a maximum performance takeoff and a few touch and goes to say thanks!

Permission was granted by the now occupied part-time tower, and they were off looking like Danny was in control. Holding the brake and revving the engine to start a quick roll, Ernie transitioned and immediately went into a near vertical climb before reaching the end of the runway, continuing the climb until 1Ducky started to stall. Ernie then dropped the left wing into a hammerhead stall and brought 1Ducky into a downwind pattern. He came in doing a barrel roll and then a touch and go, wagging his wings goodbye to a startled band of reporters and spectators. Danny was giddy with laughter. "I never knew an amfib could do that!"

"They can't. That's why I only did one!" shouted Ernie with a laugh.

"I don't think I will ever forget this, Ernie!!!"

"You shouldn't! It's one of those good times we talked about!"

THREE DAYS

Three days earlier Matt Karayan, a 17-year-old New Jersey native, was sitting on a beach blanket with his high school girlfriend, Sherry when he heard a muffled explosion. They both looked out into the ocean in time to see one of the liberty ship tankers turn into a ball of flame, followed by a violent explosion that blew the top deck of the tanker into the air. The ship did not sink and, to his surprise, he actually watched the German sub surface and fire her deck guns into the burning ship. Sherry started crying, and Matt raced to the phone at the lifeguard station. He asked the operator to connect him with the coastal patrol, Navy or Coast Guard, as there was a German sub shelling a ship off of Asbury Park. His call was met with disbelief, and the line went dead. Matt tried again with the same result and just about broke the phone when he hung it up swearing and saying, "Those Nazi's are shooting at the survivors! Those poor guys! It's terrible! Now, look at 'em. Those SOB's on the sub are waving to us, and we are not able to do anything to them. When in the heck are we going to get those subs out of here?"

HEADING BACK

As Ernie started for home, he shouted to Danny that there was a report of some survivors adrift in the ocean, and there was a request for location assistance. Did he want to help look for them?

"Of course, isn't that what we are for?" replied Danny.

"Atta boy, Danny!" stated Ernie as he swung southeast and headed 1Ducky out over Long Island Sound. They flew low between Block Island and Montauk Point and, at about 20 miles from land, spotted two injured men in a small, dirty, bullet scared blue-grey raft on the calm, green, distant eastern ocean surface. The men were waving as Ernie and Danny circled while broadcasting their location to Coast Guard and Navy channels. With lots of fuel on board, 1Ducky came in low to check the surface conditions and, with only light swells to deal with, Ernie brought her in and taxied upwind toward the poorly bandaged, oil-covered men and cut the engine to an idle.

"Ahoy. What's your condition?" Ernie asked the men.

One answered in a dry gravelly voice.

"We are both suffering from burns. Our tanker was torpedoed 3 days ago off Asbury Park. We drifted northeast. No one saw us. Need water, food, and medical help."

Ernie turned to Danny, asking, "Danny, do you have a kit in the hull?"

"Yes, Sir."

Ernie continued, "Get down there and give it to those guys. It should hold them until a boat comes. Tell them help has been called, but we will stay with them till they get here. We will climb up again to direct the rescue boats."

The men waved to them as they took off, and 1Ducky climbed to circle them some more and, in the distance, Danny could see a Coast Guard cutter heading their way. Ernie dove toward the

148

cutter and directed them to follow. The guardsmen waved and stayed on course to the raft. Once the cutter was pulling up to the side of the raft and taking the men on board, Ernie made another low pass over the cutter and headed for Tiverton

Danny exclaimed, "Man those guys were really in a lot of hurt. It was a good thing we came along. That is really another good time to remember."

Ernie just smiled at him

FOURTH PATROL

U87 was given another refitting during July and August of 1942, and by August 31st, she was back on patrol in the Eastern Atlantic looking for British convoys to and from the Mediterranean. Off of Freetown, Africa, she sunk the British freighter Agapenor and returned to port in early December 1942.

ROBERT'S BLESSING

December 6, 1942, was the Sunday D.B. scheduled with the Branners to go see Robert. She looked crisp and neat in her Red Cross Uniform and met Kay and Bill Branner in the hospital lobby. D.B. had brought Bill and Tommy along and, even though there was a hospital rule about no children visitors, she thought that the boys might enjoy the trip and get a kick out of being able to at least wave to Robert's window.

The Branners were not optimistic about Robert's condition, which had been up and down for some time. He had endured constant transfusions because of excessive bleeding from the lesions on his body. The constant pain had sapped his strength to go on, and the doctors were not optimistic. There just did not seem to be a medicine available that could turn things around for Robert.

D.B. said she was sorry and had no idea that things were so bad. The Branners said they understood and escorted her to Robert's room. As soon as he saw her, he held up his arms and D.B. embraced him while he lay on his bed in the new pajamas and bathrobe his mom had dressed him in for his anticipated visitors. Mr. and Mrs. Branner stepped out to go out to Bill and Tommy, and so D.B. could visit with Robert.

His bandages covered most of the lesions on his head, but his face had recent scars on his tender skin. Even so, his eyes brightened with the sight of D.B. Robert seemed to have a renewed strength and wanted to talk about everything D.B. knew about the Aero Gang and how Harold Tarbert and Swifty were doing. D.B. did the best she could to cover all questions and talked about how things would be when he returned.

He pulled her up short by saying, "I don't think that will happen. It has been a good flight, but I am running out of fuel and don't think I can stay aloft. I want you to know how much my memory of the gang and my family and you have meant to me. It has allowed me to carry this battle longer than I thought it would last. Promise me you will relay to the gang how much I care for them and tell them that if that Talon shows up again, to use real bombs and take her down."

"Oh, I will, Robert! And I want you to know that I admit I have a special love for you that goes beyond the difference in our years. You have always been special to me."

Robert smiled and said, "Oh how I have wanted to hear you say that because I have always felt a special bond with you too." He raised himself up on one elbow and kissed her softly on the lips and slowly settled back onto his pillow with a smile of peace and contentment.

After a long period of hand-holding silence, D.B. announced tearfully,

"Robert, you have some more visitors."

Mr. and Mrs. Branner, Bill, and Tommy walked in and stood next to Robert's bed. Robert looked up and said, "At last all that is important to me is here with me. Thank you!"

Bill said, "The doctor and the nurses felt they could make an exception to the no kids rule and let us come up for a short visit."

Tommy chimed in that perhaps they could set up the wheelchair so Robert could be at the window to wave goodbye when they leave. Robert nodded agreement and motioned to the nurse to get a chair. Robert admitted that he was really tired, so there was not much talking, but each took turns holding Robert's hand.

Bill said, "Tomorrow it will be one year since you and Danny took after that Talon sub. The gang has come a long way because of your lead, Robert. We all love and admire you and always will."

Tommy had heard the expression on the radio and added, "Godspeed, Robert!"

With that, D.B. and her two passengers left Robert's room, teary-eyed, and headed toward the lobby. Tommy ran ahead to the front sidewalk and looked up to see his Mom and Dad standing on either side of Robert waving, as promised. Everyone continued to wave until D.B., and the boys were out of sight and back in Baker for the long ride back to Tiverton.

Mr. and Mrs. Branner stayed with Robert until he passed away the next day.

His funeral was on December 12, 1942, and he would have enjoyed the formality. Though Robert was never in the military, the Wing provided a flag for his coffin, and the Aero Gang served as pallbearers as he was laid to rest in Tiverton's Pocasset Cemetery on Blueberry Hill, a place of fond memories for Robert and his family.

A DIFFICULT TIME

Each member of the Aero Gang dealt with Robert's death in his or her own way. Most just reflected on him privately and said nothing in public. Ernie did craft a plaque in Robert's memory and placed it on a post near the shoreline spot where the Wasp crashed. He also asked the Balboa Oil company to donate a small section of the shoreland to the town of Tiverton to create a small area to be known as Robert's Park. Aside from that and the formality of the funeral, there was very little public recognition of this difficult time.

For Tommy and the rest of the Branners, however, the next months were hard. Like a growing number of families who were losing loved ones in the war, the Branners were no exception. Everyone was getting ready for Christmas, but there was just no spirit in their household with Robert being gone. Mr. and Mrs. Branner frequently cried when they were together at morning breakfast and sometimes after supper and even after going to bed. Tommy could hear their crying and sad conversations. In fact, everyone's affect was continually sad.

It was the efforts of Mr. Branner's boss, Frank L. Armstead, the plant manager of the Fall River Firestone Plant, who first helped bring things around. Mr. Armstead was an always well-dressed suit and tie, cigar smoking executive who was short enough to wear lifts in his shoes. The resulting affect was a commanding presence which demanded respect that was easily returned if an employee put forth a serious effort. On the flip side, this serious at work, balding man, with, almost sad, basset hound eyes could be quite affable with a tendency to look at the positive side of things and find humor in the negative. Above all, he cared about his fellow employees. Early one morning he called Mr. Branner into his office to talk about Robert's passing.

"Bill, I am concerned about you and Kathryn and the boys."

"I appreciate that Frank," Bill responded.

"Do you think you could use some more time off?"

"No, not with the war on. Besides work is therapeutic for both Kay and me, and the neighborhood has been really supportive of Bill Jr. and Tommy. I think we will pull through this. Some families have lost more than one child."

"Just the same, I want you to talk with someone. Start with Dr. Galine, our plant doctor. He is a great doctor, and perhaps he can help you and Kathryn or recommend someone who might help you. Have you talked with your pastor, Rev. Silver? I've heard that he is a pretty good counselor and pastor."

"Yes, but he is soon leaving for the war and won't be available for long. I suppose I can talk with Dr. Galine."

"Good. I also want you to try to get out and play some golf. I know you are too good for me, but perhaps we could still play on Sundays, war permitting."

Bill, with some emotion starting to show on his face, answered, "I'd like that, but I really hope I can find something for Kay. She is really taking everything hard and doesn't want her other boys to do anything away from home."

"Bill, my wife, Hilda, knows about your loss and has offered to help. Care if I pass the baton to her for some shopping or card playing that includes Kay?"

"That would be nice, but it may take more than one request by Hilda, as Kay is rather reserved about venturing out of the home unless it is to work," Bill answered while wiping his face with his handkerchief.

Frank replied, "That's okay Bill. Hilda has a knack for finding plenty to do, especially if it involves spending my money, but she is a wonderful, well-meaning person. They could start a book club or do crafts, but the main thing is to get Kay back to being involved with the living, right?"

"Right, I hope it works. We all need to lighten up, for sure."

It did work. Hilda contacted Kay and introduced her to some friends who would get together once or twice a week. In so doing, the ladies decided to join the Red Cross, "Knit Your Bit" program, where they would knit hats, scarves, socks, mittens, and gloves for the men and women in the military. Women and young girls across the nation were involved, and it was a huge success. Locally the program served a constructive purpose while giving the ladies time to visit and was, indeed, therapeutic for Kay. The change started to show in the Branner household and the resulting happiness of Tommy and Billy, as well as Mr. Branner, served as a catalyst for Kay, and gradually the cloud of depression began to lift, though there were still recurring tears from time to time. Bill Jr. tried to get away to be with the gang, and sometimes Tommy would go along, but things just were not to ever be the same.

PACKING

The next Sunday, the 20th, after church and the Sunday dinner, Tom asked his parents if he could take a Christmas card to Toby. They thought that would be a nice thing to do and, before they could say another word, he was out the door, shouting that he would be back before supper time.

As he walked down the street, Tom saw Toby putting things into his brother's car and noticed that Toby was crying.

"Whatcha doin, Toby?

"Packing!" he sniffed, wiping his nose on his sleeve.

"You takin a trip?" Tommy continued to question.

"You might say that. My brother is driving my Mom and me to Providence to look at a boarding school for me. The students there will all be home for Christmas break, and it's supposed to be a good time to see it. So we have an appointment for a two-hour visit at St. Duncan's.

"That why you are in a suit?"

"Yea and I hate it, and I know I am going to hate boarding school."

"What is it anyways?"

"It's a school you live and eat and sleep at, and there are all kinds of rules on when to get up and when to study school work and when to play games, go to sleep and get up and how to dress, walk, talk, and be nicey nice. I know I ain't gonna like it but what can I do? The teachers at Ft. Barton say I don't go to school enough, and it is the law that I have to go to school at least until I'm 16. My folks talked to some people, and they are helping to pay for it.

"Are ya goin to be gone today?"

"No, I'm supposed to be back tonight. I will be home through Christmas, and then I go for good the day after New Year's day."

"What if ya don't like it?"

"My Dad says I hafta like it."

"You could run away."

"Yea but I can't come home if I do."

"You could live at the fort. I'd bring ya food."

Toby smiled and put his arm around Tommy.

"I know ya would, Tom, but I think they would find me there. No, if I run, it will have to be far and where no one knows me."

"Will you let me know so I can find ya sometime? "

"Yea, I'll try. Tommy."

"Thanks for coming to say goodbye."

"Here's a Christmas card I made for ya. Maybe we will be able to play some over Christmas."

"Maybe. Well, so long Tommy. Thanks for the card," Toby said, and he climbed into the back seat of his brother's Ford with his mom, as his brother and dad settled into the front seats.

Tommy ran after the car, waving till it went past his house at 67 Haskins.

Then he watched it stop at HWY 138, turn north toward Fall River, then probably to Providence.

Tommy came back into his house and flopped down in his Dad's reading chair looking sad.

"Did Toby like your card, Tommy?" his mom asked.

"I think so, but he didn't open it. He just got into his brother's car, and they drove off."

"Says he's going to see a boarding school and will be back tonight but, somehow, I don't think I will ever see him again."

"How can the Glavins afford that?" Mrs. Branner wondered out loud.

"Toby said that some people are helping him."

Bill looked up at his mom and said, "Maybe our government is making sure he doesn't talk."

"Oh, Billy. Don't think that way!" his Mom admonished. "We always need to be positive!"

"I was just thinking out loud, Ma.!" Billy said reflectively.

FALMOUTH SCORES

Robert's Wing assisted Coastal Patrol 18 just after Donald Schnell was taken off the towing duties and assigned to sub patrol sometime after Christmas 1942. It was not until 9 January 43 that possible enemy submarine activity was again suspected to be in Rhode Island waters. Since he was in Falmouth at the time, he was granted permission to fly a Fairchild 24 and head out toward Block Island. He was in the air again on the 10th and was about 50 miles south of Block Island when he spotted a sub trailing an oil slick. Aluminum marker bombs were dropped while relaying location information to the U.S.Navy and Coast Guard. The Navy ships quickly followed the directions of the Civil Air Patrol plane and sunk the U boat, but no identity of the German sub was ever established.

THE LAST PATROL

Although U 87 was never officially seen in Rhode Island waters again, there were unofficial reports of U boats off the New England and New York coasts. The East coast was in a panic from the brazen attacks on U.S. shipping by the German navy. Blackout drills were now more common as America finally realized that they were vulnerable to attack.

On one search and rescue mission far beyond Martha's Vineyard, Ernie Gibson and William Branner spotted what looked like a sub heading east into the Atlantic, away from shipping lanes. Bill Branner plotted its course, and its track looked like it might be heading directly for Gibraltar at the entrance to the Mediterranean Sea. Since it was running on the surface, there was a good chance she was in difficulty, and the two spotters informed the Navy of the sighting and possible track she was heading. No sub was located, but coincidentally, U87 was recorded as making it home to France for another resupply and was hurriedly sent out for her fifth patrol on January 9, 1943.

She was not seen again until March 4, 1943, when Captain Jamie Clarkson was anticipating action and ready to fire depth charges from his four-stack destroyer, HMCS St Croix accompanied by the Corvette, HMCS Shediac. The two Canadian ships were a part of a Canadian escort group, C-1, forming a protective ring for Convoy KMS 106 off the coast of Portugal.

There had been sonar contacts of a possible enemy submarine and periodic sightings of periscopes. U 87 had broken off from an attack on convoy UC-1 due to an oil leak. She made contact and rendezvoused with U 461, a milkcow, (service sub), for oil and temporary repairs. U 87 hurried her repairs, refueled, and headed after convoy KMS106.

Captain Bruger was a bit perplexed about U87. She had been refitted and inspected by two service subs yet, due to the vicious depth charge attacks by the American and British destroyers, still was plagued with an oil leak and persistent water leaks from the snorkel and two periscopes. Bruger had to order the snorkel removed and silently cursed that red and yellow plane that had hit his conning tower with the firebomb and chains that ripped at the radio antennas and periscopes. None had worked perfectly since that ill-fated day when his sub was almost lost in the Sakonnet River. Even though he still admired the guts and determination of the unarmed boys in the plane, he still whispered an oath, "Darn those kids!"

Bruger called his officers together and explained his plan for the coming attack.

"We have been following this convoy's track for three days, and, even though it continues to zig zag, we know that it is headed for North Africa to supply Montgomery's forces. We need to hit them before they hit Gibraltar and enter the Mediterranean. The Straights are too well patrolled by the Allies, and, besides, our Luftwaffe is assigned to that area. We are off the coast of Portugal and will need to hit the convoy before it moves in closer to the coast and shallower water. That way we will have an easier time of escaping if challenged.

Every one of the officers present nodded agreement. Bruger continued by acknowledging his leading engineer, Dieter Wilhelm, whose approval was essential if they were to continue.

"I need to emphasize that I am worried about U87 and her persistent leaking of oil out and water in. The oil leaves a trail for detection, and the water could become a problem if the pumps fail, and we have to go deep. Even at maximum depth, the oil will tell our enemy where we are, and they will persist with the charges. We have to hit quickly and hard. Their destroyers will not be expecting us to surface after torpedoing a freighter or tanker. Our Blitzkrieg will be the launching of our remaining torpedoes on the surface and engaging them with our deck cannons to keep them from firing on us. If we can take out the destroyers and any fast moving craft close by, we have a chance to escape on the surface at first and then slip under if other enemy ships or aircraft converge on us. Since our contact with the milkcow, we have had no contacts with any other U boats. We must assume that we are on our own with this convoy. Obviously, we will try to take the largest ship first and immediately be ready for the surface engagement. We need to know where the destroyers are in relation to our first target and immediately engage on the surface. Is everyone in agreement?"

Again there was a unanimous agreement but this time accompanied with a resounding, "Yes, my captain," followed by cheers and with that Bruger called for battle stations and began his early morning hunt for the largest ship. Amidst the clamor, Wilhelm shouted to Burger, "She is a tough boat sir and will serve us well and do you proud!"

Within an hour and a half the ship was about 1000 meters off port side and, as U87 closed in for the kill, Berger ordered three torpedoes fired.

"Feuer, Feuer, Feuer!" (Fire, Fire, Fire)

With the rapid surfacing, there was no time to see if the torpedoes found their mark. U87 immediately launched two more torpedoes toward the two destroyers that were turning to seek out the German U-boat.

U87's deck guns were quickly blazing amidst the explosions of depth charges as she plowed forward in a full speed surface attack.

Through his high power binoculars, Captain Clarkson saw the torpedo trails as they sped toward the largest tanker in the convoy. He scanned the surface and was shocked to see the sub surface and in a full surface attack, fire two torpedoes at the St. Croix while rapidly firing her deck guns and smaller arms.

"What a gutsy move!" he said to himself as he prepared the launching of a countering salvo of depth charges at the closing sub. The Shediac followed suit. It was as they launched their second salvo that Captain Clarkson saw the Talon emblem on the sub's conning tower. The image was quickly lost as the frothy explosions from both Canadian ships seemed to explode near their mark. U87 appeared to dive under after the second salvo. Even so, the two Canadian ships fired their third and final salvos.

Suddenly all was quiet, and Jamie looked over the surface. He saw nothing but scant debris. There were no survivors. In fact, he even wondered if the sub had simply returned to the safety of the depths on her own or was hiding under one of the convoy ships. Both Canadian destroyers were unscathed, and the tanker was still with the convoy. He concluded that the St. Croix had turned toward the sub and avoided the two torpedoes fired at her, and the first three torpedoes aimed at the tanker had either been duds or bounced off without detonating.

"What a blessing," he said with an exhausted sigh. With so little debris though, Jamie wondered if the sub had somehow fooled them all again by plowing under the destroyers and escaping by diving deep and running silent. He even chanced open communication with the rest of the convoy to see if anyone had seen or detected the sub. Since there was no supportive confirmation, he felt certain that she had gone down. That evening he routinely entered in his Captain's log his crew's efficient actions in this encounter and ended with a simple summary statement:

"German U87 (TALON SUB) down; West of Leixoes at 410.36' North and 130.31'West on 4 March 1943." A similar cable note would be sent to London, Ontario and relayed to Falmouth, Massachusetts and Tiverton, Rhode Island.

Shortly after that time, the American Navy and Coast Guard had finally geared up enough to start taking over the duties of the Civil Air Patrol. The Falmouth Coastal Patrol Base that had been activated on 25 August 1942 lost one hangar and four aircraft to a fire in September of 1943 and was closed in October of 1943 due to the fire damage. Even so, it was through the efforts of many units like Robert's Wing and the Falmouth C.A.P., that the proud German Kregsmarine was forced to withdraw most of its submarines from the American coastline in an effort to defend her own home waters. Indeed, the tide of war had changed.

For the C.A.P. men and women, like those of Robert's Wing of the Aero Gang, the war was over. There was much celebration when Germany surrendered on 9 May 1945, but the stress of war was still present because Japan was still fighting.

The real celebrations began on the night of 14 August 1945, when Japan surrendered, and, like many other Americans across the nation, Kay Branner tore down her blackout curtains and danced and sang with all the neighbors, family, and friends who had gathered in front of the Philco in the Branner living room.

Life in Tiverton returned to a more normal pace, though Robert, Toby, and Harold were no longer in the mix. Toby did well at St. Duncan's and did visit Tommy around holiday times as he had promised. Harold continued with the R.C.A.F. until war's end and stayed in Canada after he left the Air Force. William and Walter both got their wings and stayed close to Ernie until they graduated from high school. Bill went on to college in Ohio. Walter joined the Navy and was with the occupation forces in Japan. Swifty joined the Marines and flew everything ever made and was one of the first Navy aviators to fly jets. Danny graduated high school and finally became an aircraft mechanic and got a job at Hillsgrove Airport outside of Providence. Donald Schnell stayed with the Civil Air Patrol and settled in Fall River. D.B. moved to Florida, as did Bill and Caty McArdell. Ernie sold his cabinet shop and joined Bill Blunt to retire somewhere in the North Country doing occasional charter flights into Canada. After the war, Tommy and his Mom and Dad moved to Wisconsin. Tom also did eventually earn his wings while in college.

EPILOG

There was one more incident of U boat activity in Rhode Island waters as late as May 5th, 1945. On that day, the Black Point was sunk by U853 off of Newport. U853 was followed by volunteer and military aircraft and ships, depth charged and sunk.

The six-year Battle of the Atlantic was finally over. It had been won by the efforts of many, from many countries and walks of life. But no small part was played by the very real, young and old civilians, like those in the fictitious Robert's Wing, who made up the Coastal Patrol, better known by it's more common and present name, the Civil Air Patrol.

Today we are losing our World War II veterans at a rapid rate. There is not much time to learn that many who fought for our shores were not even in the military. They were volunteers like our Minute Men of the American Revolution. In this longest Battle of the War, 65 volunteer Civil Air Patrol crew members were killed, 21 due to hostile action with submarines. Another 26 were lost on Coastal Patrol operations, with the remainder due to weather and accidents. Another seven were injured. In total, 90 C.A.P. aircraft were lost. Once they were finally authorized to use depth charges and bombs in the waning months of 1942, these sacrifices yielded 173 U boat sightings, 83 bomb/depth charge attacks on 57 sub-targets with two confirmed sinkings of enemy submarines. All this was accomplished by volunteers who flew over 24 million miles in 244,600 flight hours and 86,865 hours over water missions. In addition, the Coastal Patrol/Civil Air Patrol assisted 91 ships in distress and rescued 363 lives, located 17 floating mines and flew 5684 special convoy protection missions. Not bad for a bunch of little red and yellow planes! Indeed, their efforts resulted, in no small part, to the foiling of the Axis efforts to invade and conquer North America.

History has a way of repeating itself, and we all need to take a moment and reflect on our early failures and successes, show our respect and appreciation for those who have gone before, and be prepared to volunteer ourselves when the need arises again. Just as the armed citizenry of thc Minute Men era helped defeat British domination of Rhode Island and her twelve sister states, so, too, the armed citizenry of the C.A.P. helped defeat the possibility of a more global domination. We have a right to "keep and bare arms," and we must never minimize the value of our second amendment rights! Perhaps Winston Churchill said it best when he was referring to the R.A.F. pilots; "Never has so much been owed by so many to so few."

"God Speed, C.A.P."

ABOUT THE AUTHOR

Thomas Carl Brandy is a native of Fall River, Massachusetts. He grew up in Tiverton and Barrington, Rhode Island and is a graduate of Woodstock Academy in Woodstock, Connecticut where he first discovered his love for writing. He earned his Bachelor of Arts degree in education at Heidelberg University in Tiffin, Ohio where he wrote for his school newspaper. He furthered his education with a Master's degree from the University of Wisconsin (Madison) and had additional studies at the University of Oslo (Norway) and Minnesota State (St. Cloud). He completed forty years of work in Special Education and Rehabilitation Administration throughout the mid-west. Now retired, Tom is an active senior member of the Civil Air Patrol and has resumed his interest in writing historical fiction. Robert's Wing is his first novel. He and his wife, Ingrid, and their three sons reside in the Rochester, Minnesota area.

Made in the USA
Monee, IL
13 January 2023

25190299R00100